Always Coca-Cola

A Swallow Editions Book
Founder and Series Editor: Rafik Schami

Always
Coca-Cola

by Alexandra Chreiteh

Translated from the Arabic by
Michelle Hartman

Interlink Books

An imprint of Interlink Publishing Group, Inc.
Northampton, Massachusetts

First published in 2012 by

INTERLINK BOOKS
An imprint of Interlink Publishing Group, Inc
46 Crosby Street, Northampton, Massachusetts 01060
www.interlinkbooks.com

Published as part of the Swallow Editions series.
Founder and Series Editor: Rafik Schami

Arabic text copyright © by Alexandra Chreiteh 2009, 2012
English translation copyright © by Michelle Hartman 2012
Swallow Editions symbol copyright © Root Leeb, 2011
Originally published in Arabic by Arab Scientific Publishers,
Beirut, Lebanon, 2009

Library of Congress Cataloging-in-Publication Data

Chreiteh, Alexandra.
[Da'iman Coca-Cola. English.]
Always Coca-Cola / by Alexandra Chreiteh ; translated by Michelle Hartman.
-- 1st American ed.
    p. cm.
ISBN 978-1-56656-843-2 (pbk.) -- ISBN 978-1-56656-873-9 (hardcover)
1. Young women--Lebanon--Fiction. 2. Beirut (Lebanon)--Fiction. I. Hartman, Michelle. II. Title.
PJ7918.H74D3513 2011
892.7'36--dc23
                                2011024050

Cover image Copyright © Pakmor | Dreamstime.com
Book design by Pamela Fontes-May

Printed and bound in the United States of America

To order or request our complete catalog,
please call us at 1-800-238-LINK, or e-mail: info@interlinkbooks.com

Always Coca-Cola

WHEN MY MOTHER WAS PREGNANT WITH ME, she had only one craving. That craving was for Coca-Cola.

Her burning desire for Coca-Cola was all the more powerful because it was forbidden. In addition to the fact that my father prevented her from buying it—because in his opinion it was inseparable from American policies that he opposed—he also monitored my mother's food intake with the severity of a school headmaster. He wrote down the foods and drinks forbidden to her and Coca-Cola was at the top of the list. As her pregnancy progressed, the pressure he exerted on her about the particulars of her nutritional intake increased until it had transformed into something of an obsession—he especially used to scrutinize the specific type of water that she would drink; tap water was completely off limits because it was polluted. He was afraid that dirt in the tap water would travel to the fetus in her belly and leave behind a residue, and so he started buying her purified, bottled water from a man who passed through the neighborhood once a week, even though it was really expensive because this was during the war. He wanted this baby to be born clean and pure—completely flawless—exactly like the water that he paid dearly for.

He had a subconscious philosophy about all of this: pure water guarantees that a baby will be naturally predisposed to cleanliness and this will remain part of the child's innate nature after birth. The mother's nourishment profoundly affects the fetus! The months spent in the womb are a decisive period in a human being's existence! Any error a mother commits during this time affects a child's psychological and physical constitution forever.

Therefore, my father wanted to ensure that I would have a natural, and permanent, predisposition for cleanliness.

One hot summer's day, around noon, the sun was beating down on the eastern side of our house and my mother was craving Coca-Cola. There was an electricity cut and this meant that all of the air conditioners shut off; the intense heat turned my mother's face red and beads of sweat were forming on her upper lip. She was exhausted, nearly at the end of her pregnancy. The heat was unbearable and my mother felt the baby moving inside her with a force that she wasn't used to, so she sat down on a low chair, leaning back to relieve the pressure from her belly that was swollen with me. Then she opened her legs, lifting up the hem of her dress to expose her scorching thighs, in an attempt to cool them off, saying to my father with a sigh, "I want Coca-Cola. Bring me Coca-Cola."

My father didn't answer because he too was feeling the stifling heat and when she insistently repeated her request, he shouted right in her face, "Where can I get you a Coke now? Drink water!"

"I'm so thirsty... Bring me a Coke!"

There's no doubt that the thirst that overtook my mother at that moment was seriously strong. No, there's no doubt that it shook her entire being beyond what she could endure, because this craving of hers left an indelible imprint on me: I was born with a small birthmark that looks like a little Coca-Cola bottle, on my upper back, right between my shoulder blades. My mother sees this birthmark whenever I get undressed in front of her; it is a reminder of her unquenched thirst.

I remembered this incident because I had been searching for a company to take me on as a trainee for a short period of time and my friend Yana volunteered to ask her boyfriend, the manager of the Coca-Cola factory, if he could help. It's really very difficult to get work at this company, but the manager can't refuse any request of hers.

Yana's plan of action was as follows: to visit her boyfriend at his office and then to come to my house and tell me the answer at exactly five in the evening; this was the best time for her to come since no one in my family would be home then, meaning that we could feel free to do as we please. I was really hoping that my friend would have the influence to get this job for me because it's one of the prerequisites of my degree and I cannot graduate from university this year without it.

But Yana was very late for our appointment—it got to be five-thirty and she hadn't come yet, which was strange since she's not usually late for her appointments. I started worrying about her, especially after I called her a bunch of times, first on her mobile phone and then on her landline, and she didn't answer. I wondered what could have made her so late and I started to get anxious.

I decided to occupy myself with something, so I took a cardboard box full of women's magazines out from under my bed, picked one out and started flipping through it. A short article about how important it is for women to use lip balm caught my attention. In it, the writer claimed that fashion models don't ever leave home without using a high-SPF lip balm to protect them from harmful outdoor elements like sun and dust. It's extremely important for models to protect their lips because the lips are the most important symbol of a woman's femininity and attractiveness. Lip balm helps them protect their lips from dryness and chafing and thereby also protects their femininity. But reading the article didn't put a stop to my worrying. I had to find something else to do until Yana came, so I decided to pop out to the pharmacy near my house and buy lip balm.

I left my house, crossed Mar Elias Street and went into the pharmacy right next door to my father's flower shop. The pharmacist knows my father very well and knows that I'm his daughter, so he smiled at me when I entered and sold me the balm at a discount. I put some on my lips and as I left, wondering as I did so whether Yana uses the very same balm to protect her lips.

Outside, a sandstorm had begun to gather speed, but I walked confidently into the dusty wind, believing that my lips were well protected by this balm. But the balm didn't protect my lips, on the contrary, dust started to build up on them! Even worse, I licked my lips in an attempt to remove the dust but it stuck to my tongue, forcing me to swallow it because girls don't spit in the street.

When I returned to my building's entrance, I was surprised to see Yana. She had arrived while I was at the pharmacy and our friend Yasmine was with her. I wondered why Yasmine was there, but Yana sidetracked me by telling me two crucially important pieces of information: the first was that she had lost her passport. And the second was... that she might be pregnant... but she's not sure yet.

"I'm not sure yet!" she said, with artificial calm.

"Let's go to the pharmacy right now and buy you a pregnancy test, so that you can be sure," responded Yasmine, whose face betrayed no sign of shock.

I stopped at the corner of the building's entrance and pretended to be busy tying my shoelace so that they would go to the pharmacy without me. I was afraid that the pharmacist would tell my father that I had bought a pregnancy test, even though the test wasn't for me. I knew my father well enough to know that if he learned about this he would cut my throat with the pregnancy test before he would even let me tell him the whole story. So I couldn't risk going into the pharmacy; instead, I hid myself completely while keeping an eye out for my father, for fear that he would decide to visit his friend the pharmacist at this very moment. If he entered the pharmacy and saw my friends doing what they were doing, it would be me who would feel his anger. Isn't he the one who always says, "Tell me who your closest friends are, and I will tell you who you are!"

But I felt reassured when I saw him busily putting the flowers displayed outside for sale back inside his shop, afraid that the wind, heavy with dust, would kill them. I also noticed the new sign above the shop's entrance that my father had hung yesterday in place of the old one, which had been eaten by rust, completely obliterating the name of the shop. He rewrote the same old name on the new sign, though I had asked—and even begged—him to change it. He had refused my request, however, insisting on keeping the name that I hate so much!

This name is: Abeer Ward. Fragrant Rose.

My father thought up the name of his shop when he opened it twenty-five years ago and he was so thrilled with it that when I was born he named me

Abeer (fragrance), so that the shop and I had the very same name: Abeer Ward—our family name is also Ward (rose). It seems that this name was bestowed on my father's grandfather a long time ago because he sold flowers. This profession was passed down in the family through the generations until it arrived at my father, who transformed it from a profession into a whole life philosophy.

I always ask him: How could you name your only daughter after your shop?

So I don't like my name and I believe that it doesn't suit me in the least. For my whole life, I've been waiting to reach legal age so that I could change it. But when I finally turned eighteen, I realized that I had neither enough money to cover the full cost of court fees, nor enough patience to undertake all of the required legal proceedings. In all of this, the most important thing is that my father—the moment I let him know about my plan—forbade me unequivocally from changing it because my name is the most beautiful name that a young lady could possibly have, in his opinion.

And thus I lost hope that I could exchange Abeer Ward, Fragrant Rose, for another name. I surrendered myself to this reality, thinking that whenever I get married I can exchange my family name for my husband's. Then I started constantly wondering, when it happens, what name will be my destiny? Will I turn into Abeer... What? Abeer Helou, Sweet Fragrance? Abeer Zaki, Delightful Fragrance?

I don't know and I'm in no rush to get married. It's too soon!

I hadn't realized the extent to which I had surrendered myself to my own thoughts until my friends returned from the pharmacy and Yasmine surprised me with her question, "Who are you hiding from in the corner?"

But I didn't answer, seeing that Yana was hurrying toward the elevator. She stopped in front of it and pushed the call button—I understood from this that she wanted to do her pregnancy test in my house, of all places! This made me nervous because I knew how dangerous this could be for me: someone from my family could come back unexpectedly, realize what was going on and we would be busted. But before I could formulate an objection and ask Yana to go anyplace other than my house, the elevator came, we got in it and it took us up without one word crossing my lips.

When we arrived at the third floor, where I live, I opened the apartment door reluctantly. Yana ran to the bathroom, slamming the door so loudly that it echoed in my head for a while. Yasmine hurried to follow her but I stopped her saying, "Oof! Let her breathe a little!"

Yasmine did as I asked and left Yana to sort herself out in the bathroom alone. The two of us sat down on one of the sofas in the living room. With a mechanical movement, Yasmine turned on the television and asked, "If she's really pregnant, who do you think the baby's father is?"

This question surprised me even though it was relevant—the father could be one of two people: either Yana's ex-husband, from whom she had been separated for a short time, or her boyfriend, the manager of the Coca-Cola factory. These are the only two men Yana knew in Lebanon.

(Yana never said, "Lebanon," but rather always referred to the country with the English expression, "the land flowing with milk and honey," because that's what her illustrated tourist guide calls it.)

Yana is Romanian. She came to Lebanon with her ex-husband, who worked as an employee in a trade corporation that used to send him to Romania from time to time. He met her on one of these visits and they married a few months later and then moved together to Beirut. Yana was really enthusiastic about the move. She had always felt something inside her pulling her toward deserts, palm trees, and mirages and she was sure that she would find all that here. She came expecting to see naked women swaying to eastern melodies, with their heads and faces (except for the eyes) covered, in ornamented castles with gold-plated bathrooms, in the depths of which dancing slave girls were hidden. She especially dreamed of her husband the prince's royal court, where he would sit on pillows made of fine silk and the softest feathers, and she would sit beside him.

But this prince of hers, in reality, lives in one of those "old rental" apartments on Hamra Street, above none other than Starbucks. Yana didn't find the desert here, but just a lot of dust that she had to wipe up every morning. As for the dancing slave girls, she only saw them in foreign films translated into Arabic. In their place (much to her surprise!), she saw women wearing bikinis at the beach, where she went only once because she found out that the soft, golden sand pictured in her travel guide was actually covered with the glass of broken bottles and used needles. As for the water in whose azure depths she had dreamed of swimming, it was full of jellyfish that looked like plastic bags or plastic bags that looked like jellyfish. To top it all off, only minutes after arriving at the beach, a group of young men approached her and asked, in English, "How much?"

Angered by this deflated hope, she burned the books of Omar Khayyam, the collections of Mutanabbi's poetry and the English translation of the *1001 Nights*—books that had been a gift from her husband when she came to Beirut to live with him there permanently.

That day, Yana realized that she did not love her husband, but merely had been enamored with the idea of traveling to a faraway country—he had been nothing but a means to help her realize this dream. Their relationship quickly worsened, to the point that Yana was sure that she could no longer stay married to him. So she called a lawyer and asked for a divorce. She and her husband agreed that he would leave her the house and that he would move to another neighborhood in Beirut—above a restaurant called "Ali Baba and the Forty Chickens." Many months had passed since their separation and she had not seen him since then, but she was still legally his wife because the divorce proceedings were not yet completed and were not progressing at the speed that Yana would have desired.

This separation had backed her into a corner, since she had become responsible for supporting herself and had to find work quickly. This was not as easy as she had imagined or hoped, since the heavens do not rain jobs down on Beirut. But the winds of fate were blowing in her direction and landed her on the doorstep of a modeling agency. She walked in and walked out shortly after with a contract in hand. The very next day, the agency called her and said that the Coca-Cola Company had chosen none other than her to appear in one of its advertisements. She met the company's manager during the shoot for the ad; they clicked at this first meeting just like two pieces of a puzzle that complete each other, in perfect harmony.

That's what Yana thought, at least.

At that moment, Yana became certain that everything that had happened to her—from her arrival in Lebanon to her marriage and even her divorce—had not one drop of coincidence about it, indeed all of this was "written for her" long before she was even born.

This was her destiny: to cast down her anchor in Lebanon and live here forever.

For it was in Lebanon that she met her great love, nay, her other half, the person for whom she was born and who was born for her, as she always declares. Her incomplete soul had been lost and miserable for the entire twenty-four years of her life and finally fate had led her to him, as the winds guide ships at sea.

Yana has never asked me for my opinion about her relationship. But if she ever does, I'll tell her that she needs to break up with him straight away and go back to her husband for sure; marriage is not underwear that you take on and off and change every day! I actually hoped that Yana would be pregnant—but by her husband—because this would perhaps be her last chance to save her marriage. When I related my wish to Yasmine, she replied, "Who told you she wants that?"

Then she reminded me that Yana has not seen her husband since they separated, that is to say for almost six months, and she never even mentions him—it's as if he wasn't previously a part of her life. On the other hand, she talks about her boyfriend the manager every other minute as though he were the only man she knew!

I interrupted her angrily, saying, "Let's wait for the results of the test first!"

To change the subject, I asked Yasmine if she knew anything about this pregnancy test and she explained to me how easy it was to use: it consists of a plastic stick about as long and wide as a finger, or a little bit longer. In the middle of this stick there's a white paper rectangle that changes color when it reacts to the woman's urine, to let her know if she's pregnant or not. If she's not pregnant, the (-) symbol appears on the white paper, and if she is pregnant, a (+) symbol appears.

"It's really easy to use!" Yasmine assured me again and then added, "But the results are not always accurate."

I asked myself how she knew all this.

But I didn't dare ask her and she didn't volunteer an explanation, so the two of us stayed sitting silently in front of the television. Suddenly, a commercial for a condom came on and it caught my attention because I had never seen such a thing in all my life. I turned up the volume a little bit to hear it better, but a truck was passing at that same moment and honked its horn, drowning out the television so I didn't hear any of the commercial.

A few minutes later, I left Yasmine alone in the living room and headed toward the bathroom to check on Yana. I found her sitting on the toilet, head bowed, so that her black hair covered her face, like a hijab. I found the resemblance between hair and hijab quite amusing because it was so incompatible with the sight of her naked legs. I would have laughed had I not been aware that this was no time for laughter.

It was hard for me to believe that things like this could happen in the lives of ordinary people, since I had only seen such things in films... or dreams! Bad dreams, of course.

And I felt like I really was dreaming when the (+) symbol appeared on the paper rectangle, meaning that

Yana was indeed pregnant! I felt suddenly nauseated by how strange this all was to me.

Or rather I felt like someone had slapped me hard across the face and roused me from a deluded deep slumber!

Yasmine entered the bathroom and asked about the result of the test. Yana answered that she was pregnant, just as she'd expected, and without anyone asking her, she added, "I've decided to keep the baby!"

Yasmine said bluntly, "Have you lost your mind?! What about your job? Have you ever seen a fat, pregnant fashion model? Ever in your whole life?"

Yana told her that she actually had seen a lot of pregnant fashion models before, they modeled fashions for women who were pregnant, like themselves, and she added that she'd heard of fat models wearing plus-sized fashions. Yasmine, however, ignored Yana's answer completely and said, "If you don't have enough money for an abortion, I can easily get it for you!"

Yana sighed, resting her hand on her smooth, level belly, and answered, "It's not a question of money! It's every woman's dream to have the baby of the man she loves and I love him so much!"

With that, I was certain that the father of the child was not Yana's ex-husband as I had led myself to believe and hope for, but was her boyfriend—the manager of the Coca-Cola factory—exactly as Yasmine had predicted, and I had feared, it would be.

I said nothing and Yasmine herself was silent, but Yana added, "Furthermore, I believe in qadar. I am convinced that getting pregnant by him is qadari ou nasibi!"

Yana said qadari ou nasibi, my fate and fortune, in Arabic even though English is the language we use to communicate. In the past few weeks, her use of this expression had reached obsessive levels: if anyone said anything to her, no matter how trivial, she would immediately respond, without hesitating, "This is qadari ou nasibi."

I believe that she heard this expression in some song and memorized it, because she frequently repeats things in a lot of Lebanese songs, like:

"Only you habibi, you're qadari ou nasibi!" or

"You know you're maktubi, you're qadari ou nasibi!"

Yana listens to these songs with rapt attention and concentration and through them is trying to learn spoken Lebanese Arabic, which she aspires to master as quickly as possible because this will facilitate communication between her and her boyfriend; she always says that good communication is one of the characteristics of a successful relationship and one of the guarantees that the relationship will end in marriage!

Yana's greatest dream is exactly this; she thinks that it's merely a question of time, nothing else, before her boyfriend will ask for her hand in marriage. She is perpetually getting ready for the big moment and she mentions this to us every time she goes to see him, saying, "He's going to ask me to marry him today; everything in me feels it!"

But not once have these feelings of hers been warranted—her boyfriend never mentions the subject of marriage. This doesn't cause her to lose hope, however. On the contrary, her expectation of marriage remains firm and strong and she's convinced that with time she'll zero in on her objective!

And she now thinks that she will finally triumph because her pregnancy will settle the question at last. Once he knows that she's going to be the mother of his child, her boyfriend won't put off marriage any longer, but will ask for her hand on the spot without hesitation, change of heart or delay! This pregnancy, sent down to her from the heavens, was like a fast-forward button; she pushed it to speed up the tape and shorten her waiting time.

"Just a minute!" Yasmine said, pushing the pause button to stop the tape.

"Just a minute! Have you forgotten that you can't get married again before you've finalized your divorce and completely closed the door on your first marriage? And are you totally sure that he will even acknowledge his paternity of this child?"

Yana's face instantly started trembling and it seemed clear that Yasmine's remark had really shaken her, rocking her very foundations—indeed, it did away with these foundations all together. Yasmine had demolished the castle that Yana had built in the clouds, shattering it and scattering it in little bits all around her. But despite the blow that she had already delivered, Yasmine did not stop her violent attack and finished it off by saying, "In any case, you have to be sure that you are pregnant first, these tests are not totally accurate and might give a totally wrong result!"

"And what do you propose as a solution…?" asked Yana in a barely audible voice.

"The ideal solution," Yasmine said, "is that Yana go to the gynecologist because he alone can settle the question of whether or not she is pregnant." None of us knew a doctor, so we went to look up the address of a clinic in the phone book. We found one in Achrafiyé, which is exactly what we wanted because Achrafiyé is far from my family's house and the places that they work and always go to. We called the clinic and made an appointment for Yana for the morning of the following day.

Yana then had nothing to do but to wait for the following day to know if the test result was right or wrong. I could sense that my friend was really stressed out, because she said that the coming hours would be longer than all eternity! So I had to find a way to distract her from thinking about being pregnant until her doctor's appointment. I suggested that we all go to Starbucks. Yana liked this idea and said yes happily. Yasmine, however, wavered at first, then agreed to join us after Yana pressured her—but not for more than half an hour because it was almost time for her to go to the gym.

Yasmine agreed to go with us on the condition that we first go to her house to get her gym clothes; and we agreed because she was driving us to

Starbucks in her car. Yasmine lives by herself in an apartment that she rented in the Snoubra area, close to our university, LAU, like many students who come to Beirut from faraway areas. Yasmine came to Beirut from the mountains, where she lived with her parents before she started university. Now she lives in the city permanently and rarely sees her parents. She doesn't even talk about them much, but I know that her mother is German—which is really obvious because of her foreign-looking features and especially her skin color, which is so white that Yana sometimes calls her *milk* in English!

Yasmine absolutely can't stand it when Yana calls her this—she hates any allusion to the whiteness of her skin. This name is totally perfect for her, however, because she is white like clean, new snow! Her whiteness is the most beautiful thing about her—the rest is actually somewhat ugly. This is because she doesn't take care of her "natural assets"—she doesn't put kohl around her eyes and she doesn't comb and style her hair, instead she just cuts it very short and likes to keep it like that. She isn't convinced that paying a little attention to herself could only help and not harm, so whenever I've tried to persuade her that she needs to tend to her appearance and femininity, even just a little bit, she always answers tensely, "I have much more important things to do!"

For her, the most important thing is her rigorous workout regimen. She has chosen the strangest and most violent of all sports—boxing. Personally, I don't understand what made her choose boxing: it's the kind of sport that strips a young woman of her most important attribute, her femininity. I've tried to convince her that she should do any other sport, because women aren't born for violence and physical fighting, it goes completely against their nature, they should be soft and tender like the jasmine flower of my friend's name! This is especially true of Yasmine's body, which is so white that any bump, no matter how minor, leaves a mark on it. Boxing exposes you to powerful punches, which cover your body in blue bruises—extremely ugly, even on a boy's body: so just imagine them all over the body of a young woman like Yasmine!

Then again, Yasmine's body is not in the least a woman's body: her shoulders are broad, her chest is as flat as a board, her hips are thin and taut and prominent muscles are visible on her arms. Her body doesn't contain even one ounce of femininity—any young man in his right mind would dream of having a body like hers!

For these reasons, I always try to convince her to quit boxing as quickly as possible and before it's too late, that is to say before her body is no different than a man's (except in a few small details) and it's too late for her to regain her original femininity. At that time she will have reached the point of no return, all her bridges will be burned and she will remain deformed until the end of her days. I use all kinds of logic and reason to convince her, but she is never convinced. She even told me that there wasn't an iota of logic in my words. So I had to resort to other means to make her see my point of view. I tried to scare her by reporting rumors I had heard about her at the university—for example, many people say that she's a *lesbian* and others call her butch! But Yasmine doesn't care about any of this, she isn't upset or afraid, indeed she listens to me tell her this gossip as though she were listening to the daily weather report and not to rumors that might mar her good reputation. And she keeps on pursuing her sport as though it's nothing and she was born for it: as though boxing were a religious ritual that she performs to ensure her place in heaven.

Personally, I'm embarrassed to be seen with her too much and this doesn't mean that I don't really love her—in fact the opposite is true—because she's my very best friend after Yana. But I don't want anyone to think that I am eccentric like her simply because she's my friend. So I try to meet her in obscure or remote places, far from the eyes of the crowd, like at my house or Yana's house, for example. I particularly keep my distance from her at the university, in case one of those people who ridicule her sees me. I also avoid going to her house, for this very same reason, especially as the building that she lives in is as strange as she is or perhaps even a bit stranger. I only go there in cases of extreme necessity because I distrust its residents; because of them, I feel that the place isn't "clean" and I am afraid of one of them in particular.

I'm afraid of a man who's always standing at the entrance of the building as though he's waiting for someone, but that someone never comes. When I asked Yasmine about him once she told me that his name is Waleed and that he stands at the entrance every day, without exception, even during vacations and holidays. He blocks it with his giant frame, making it impossible for anyone to pass without him granting them space because he's double the size of a normal man. It's obvious that Waleed isn't a normal man, or even a man at all—which is why even looking at him bothers me so much. Despite his enormous size, femininity just oozes out of him, the way Coca-Cola overflows out of a bottle that's been shaken before it's opened! Everything about him is always well groomed and neat, carefully and meticulously plucked; his face is covered by a thick layer of makeup and he wears a finely embroidered satin dressing gown with open-toed pumps that display the vivid shade of red painted on the toenails of his giant feet! The first time that I saw Waleed, he still had traces of stitches that seemed to be the result of unhealed wounds on his huge nose and broad jaws, no doubt resulting from an operation he had undergone not long before.

Waleed was standing in the entrance as usual when we arrived at Yasmine's building that afternoon. As soon as I saw him I told my friend that I wouldn't go up to her place with her, but would wait for her in the car, and Yana said that she would wait with me.

After Yasmine left us, Yana mentioned that she was supposed to meet my cousin Hala earlier in the day but she had gotten so taken up with this business of being pregnant that she wasn't paying attention and actually forgot all about it!

Yana and my cousin Hala do not have a close friendship, a strong friendship or really any kind of relationship at all: they have only met two or three times at most, at my house. But Hala's wedding will take place in two months and she has invited Yana because she considers it a great honor to have a foreign fashion model who appeared in a Coca-Cola ad attend her wedding. Yana had volunteered to take Hala today to her favorite tailor so that she could have her wedding dress made by him and get a discount.

At that moment Yana was about to call Hala to apologize and I feared that she would tell her the reason she was too busy for their date. This is a big risk for me because Hala has a long, wagging tongue and the news of Yana's pregnancy would reach my parents faster than email, indeed it would soon reach every member of my family—even those who live abroad!

In order to prevent this disaster, I asked Yana to let me call Hala myself and without giving her a chance to reply, I took out my mobile phone, called my cousin and told her in Arabic that the reason Yana didn't show up at their appointment is that she had suddenly been taken ill and was forced to stay in bed. When I finished the call, Yana told me that she's thrilled to attend the wedding because she's really interested in Lebanese customs and traditions and one of her dreams is to attend an authentic, native Lebanese wedding—this is why Hala's invitation had filled her with indescribable joy.

Then she added that, despite her joy, she had not forgotten to ask Hala not to serve tabbouleh at the wedding... under any circumstances! This is because Yana suffers from a severe allergy to tabbouleh—something that she discovered when she was invited to dinner at our house to taste typical Lebanese food, when she first came to live in Lebanon. This is the only dish that she ate that evening—not only because it was the only one that allowed her to watch her weight—but also because I had insisted on the importance of tabbouleh among the wide variety of Lebanese dishes. But no sooner had she finished what was on her plate than she began to have extreme difficulty breathing and we rushed her to the hospital, where they told us that she was in grave danger and that if we had waited even a little bit longer to bring her in she would have died. They performed all of the necessary tests and the doctor's opinion was that she should stop eating tabbouleh altogether.

I for one found the affair of Yana's allergy strange because she isn't allergic to any of the ingredients of tabbouleh on their own, in fact she has no problem eating parsley, the same goes for bulgur wheat, tomatoes, lemon... but when all of these ingredients are mixed together in one dish, it becomes a lethal combination!

When my cousin Hala—the bride—asked Yana the reason for her strict boycott of tabbouleh, she replied, "The best means of assassinating me is to feed me tabbouleh!" She had learned the Arabic word "assassinate" recently, because of widespread explosions in Beirut, and she used it whenever the opportunity arose. Then she added, "If I die in Lebanon, it will be because of tabbouleh! If you don't want your wedding to turn into a wake, get rid of it right away. But tabbouleh and me, we won't meet in the same place ever again!"

Right away, Hala hurried to take tabbouleh off of her wedding menu, because Yana's attendance was more important to her.

I asked Yana, "How can it be a Lebanese wedding without tabbouleh?"

But Yana didn't answer because Yasmine came back just then and we all set off for Starbucks, which we found jampacked with university students, talking and studying for their upcoming exams. Many of them were students from our university and I regretted having gone there with Yasmine. These students had occupied all but one of the tables and we rushed to take it before someone else got there. This table was in a dark corner of the café near a long sofa where a girl and boy were stretched out and lost in total abandon, making out without stopping to rest or even take a breath. The boy's abundance of ardor made him seem as though he were searching for something that he had lost in the girl's mouth. I was really embarrassed watching the two of them go at it and I turned my back to them. As for my two friends… they acted completely normally, as though nothing were happening.

As soon as we settled down at our table, Yasmine seemed really anxious, and not only did she not calm down, but she also kept busy by looking at her watch, as a clear sign that she was counting the minutes until Yana would release her. Yana noticed this and said, "Stay with us! Do you work out even on the first day of your period?"

Yasmine replied angrily, "I don't let my period prevent me from boxing!"

I thought: She really is crazy! How can she do that during her period? These are two things that don't go together, since for most women period pains are really powerful and totally incapacitate the body. Yasmine therefore must truly have ice in her veins— going to boxing practice during her period is a sign that her body doesn't feel anything. It's completely anaesthetized, like a sick body lying in the operating room!

I didn't say one word of this to Yasmine, though, because I knew she wouldn't listen to me.

All this talk of menstruation reminded me that my period was also due today and that since yesterday I'd been feeling that it was just about to come on: my breasts swelled up so that my bra almost couldn't hold them and they'd gotten rock hard. I had also started to feel a slight pain low down in my now swollen belly.

As time passed, this pain grew increasingly serious and by the time we got to Starbucks it had become acute. I decided to take painkillers as I always do, but I realized that I'd forgotten them at home because I was so distracted by Yana's pregnancy. I also forgot to bring sanitary pads. Now this really upset me, because that sharp pain is the sign that the blood will flow out of me at any second—and it will flow violently, like water pouring out of a broken faucet that you can't stop! I had to find a pad to protect my underwear as soon as possible, so that the blood wouldn't leak out onto my clothes and leave a stain on my rear end!

But finding a sanitary pad was no simple matter, since there isn't a single store nearby where I could buy them and my two girlfriends are of no use to me in this. They don't carry pads in their purses because they use tampons. But I figured that it doesn't hurt to ask, even if it doesn't help, so I asked if either of them had an Always (we call all pads "Always," even though it's the name of a specific brand).

Yasmine's answer was exactly what I expected: she said that she hadn't used Always for a long time. Then she added that when she did, she felt as though she were wearing diapers! Yana agreed and added that using sanitary pads was actually unsanitary, because blood-filled pads are the dream-come-true of all bacteria; they're like a luxuriant heaven for germs. On top of it all, pads give off an unbearable odor that can be smelled distinctly from meters away! When she walks down the street, Yana said, she smells many unpleasant odors, but sanitary pads give off the most disgusting smell of all—she can tell just by smelling whether a woman walking by is wearing one!

Yana followed up by asking me how I could stand the filth of sanitary pads, but before I could answer, Yasmine commented that she does not understand how I can use them today, because using them in this day and age is like riding a camel down a road intended for cars!

I replied to these questions jokingly, "But I always use Always!"

We all burst out laughing, but then instantly grew silent when a café worker came over to our table and asked for our order, something that Starbucks workers don't usually do. He addressed his question to Yana alone, looking only at her. He disregarded Yasmine and me as though we were nonexistent, nothing but a mere "mirage" appearing before him.

What a jerk! I said to myself.

I grumbled to express my annoyance at this jerk, but he didn't even notice me and kept staring at Yana, who smiled at him and asked for three pieces of cake as though nothing were wrong. When he asked her if she wanted to drink something, she hesitated. She said that she was afraid to drink coffee in the evening because it would make her anxious all night long, and the only drinks that Starbucks offers are various coffees and one kind of lemon juice that she really hates. He told her that he would bring her a soda even though the café's rules forbade it; he would put it in a coffee mug so that no one would notice. She was open to the idea and he asked her what kind of drink she wanted, but before she could answer he suggested, "Pepsi?"

She shook her head no, saying, "Surely not Pepsi—Coke!"

At that moment I said in English in a loud voice, "*Always, always Coca-Cola!*"

My joke cracked my girlfriends up because they knew about my urgent need for an Always pad. The server, who didn't get the loaded meaning of what I said, didn't laugh at all—he thought that I was just repeating the slogan emblazoned on every single Coca-Cola product. He went right away to bring Yana her order.

When he was a reasonable distance away from our table, Yasmine suggested that I use a tampon as she and Yana do, instead of a sanitary pad. She didn't give me the least opportunity to offer an opinion or objection but instantly produced an open box of tampons from her purse, shoving it at me until it practically touched my nose. The tampons were lined up in the box just like cigarettes lined up in a packet and I imagined that she was offering me a cigarette and not a tampon. But I declined to take one, despite her insistence, and she said, "Please don't tell me that you're afraid it'll pop your cherry if you put it inside yourself!"

She said this very loudly and I asked her to lower her voice because I was afraid that someone sitting nearby would hear us, then I whispered to her that using a tampon would for sure devirginize me—this is a fact that no one can disagree with!

After a moment's quiet, I then added in an almost inaudible voice, "But this is the least of my worries!" Yasmine said, "Then take one and stop making such a show of your chastity!" She pushed the box toward me a second time and when no comment emerged from me, she took one out to give me, at which point I noticed that it looked a lot like a suppository!

But I didn't take it from her—at that very instant I remembered that there's a machine that sells sanitary pads on the wall of the café's bathroom. I got up immediately and headed towards it—just as the hero in an American film who's in the middle of the desert heads for an oasis that's suddenly appeared to him just one or two seconds before he dies of heat exhaustion and dehydration. The oasis that I was heading for— i.e., the Starbucks bathroom—also crossed my mind at just the right time, i.e., just a few minutes before my period began.

The moment I entered the oasis/bathroom I went up to the machine and put a coin in it, so that in exchange it would spit out a sanitary pad and I could relax. But the machine didn't spit anything out; instead it spat in my face because it was broken! I said to myself, what I thought was an oasis was merely a mirage! So what should I do now? Should I wait for an Always pad to fall from the heavens like rain, or a white dove, flapping its wings that keep the moisture from leaking out onto my clothes?

But I decided to take some initiative, and so I hit the broken machine with my fist, hoping that would make a pad come out without my having to put in a coin. But the indifferent machine didn't respond to my hitting it; the only result was a sharp pain in my hand. While I was rubbing my hand to alleviate this pain, I noticed two more machines that I hadn't seen in there before, hanging on the wall near the one for sanitary pads.

On one of them was written: *Tampons 500 LL.*

And on the other: *Condoms 1000 LL.*

Seeing the second machine really disturbed me, but I was distracted from it by other more pressing and urgent concerns. At that moment, my period started. I felt a strong spasm in my lower belly and something hot starting to move between my thighs and I went into one of the stalls and discovered a huge bloodstain that had just seeped into my underwear. Fine threads branched off from the blood, looking just like rivers in an atlas, as they split off and flow into lakes. I was worried because I knew when I saw this that it was the harbinger of the coming flood and I had no bulwark against the river of blood that would flow out of me at any moment. But then all of a sudden I thought—all rivers must stop at the sea, and I sat on the toilet seat so that the blood would flow into it and not onto my clothes. Then I realized that I was stuck and could no longer get off of the seat to secure a sanitary pad, and after a few long minutes I felt that my rear end had been soldered onto the toilet and couldn't be detached.

My seat was directly across from the toilet door, which was covered in lots of scribbles that girls who had been here before me had written on it. Most of these were names and dates, or expressions of eternal love, and even sometimes other kinds of love, like the one written in English:

Dany fucked me!

This particular expression was painted on the door in nail polish that had not yet dried, so it must have been written just a few minutes earlier. I wondered: Who could have written it? But at that moment the pain in my uterus increased and I wondered instead: Will some relief come so I can get out of here?

After a few minutes this relief did come. When one of the girls from the café came into the bathroom, I opened the door of the toilet stall, stretched my head outside it and asked her for a sanitary pad even though I didn't know her. She gave me a pad, I attached it and then left immediately, wondering the whole time: Will she write something on the toilet door too when she's all alone in there?

Walking the short distance between the bathroom and our table, I tried to work out the identity of the person who wrote those words on the bathroom door. I stared at the faces of all the girls as though I expected this to be stamped in huge letters on the forehead of the one responsible, but it was the opposite of what I thought, all of their faces were free of any signs of their owners' actions or intentions. They all wore light foundation so their faces looked like clean pages, free of any letters or marks; they were as immaculate as the cleanest, clearest purified water.

When I arrived back at our table, Yasmine had already left and Yana was sitting alone, lost in thought. She didn't notice me until I asked her what she was thinking about. She answered that she had decided to tell her boyfriend about the pregnancy; she had called him while I was in the bathroom and asked him to come to see her right away. We left the café in a bit of a hurry so that Yana wouldn't be late to meet him, and when we reached the entrance to her building, she asked me to come up to her apartment with her. She didn't wait for me to answer but grabbed my hand and dragged me behind her, keeping hold of me until we had arrived at the landing in front of her apartment, at which point she had to let go of my hand to open the door.

The tiles in Yana's apartment were all torn up; this was one of the manifestations of the extreme transitional phase that it was passing through. She had decided to renovate it completely as soon as her husband moved out and left it to her. The apartment wasn't suitable for habitation because everything in it was old and damaged, beginning with the worn out, rusted pipes, which Yana was now replacing with new ones, up to and including the Arabic-style toilet, which she had never liked because of the foul smell that emanated from it. She was replacing it with another Western-style toilet and bidet, since she didn't consider it civilized for people to take care of their needs in a hole in the ground.

This renovation process was nowhere near completion six months later: the apartment was still full of piles of rubble and debris; it wouldn't be ready to emerge from all this mess for a long time still.

A few minutes after we entered the apartment, the doorbell rang and Yana opened the door to her boyfriend. This was the first time I had met him. The very moment I laid eyes on him, I thought: He's not suited to Yana, nor is she suited to him. They are absolutely different in every way; they are as different as parsley and lemon, or tomato and bulgur wheat! They can never be compatible because mixing them will create a poisonous substance—as deadly as the tabbouleh mixture is for Yana!

I don't know exactly what it was that made me think this the second I saw him.

As for him, he didn't see me when he first entered the apartment because he immediately drew Yana toward him and started kissing her passionately. After a few moments, Yana freed herself from his arms and came over to me, to introduce us. The second he knew who I was, he said that I could start work at the Coca-Cola Company in two days, no problem. I was really surprised, I wasn't expecting things to happen so quickly or easily! I thought to myself: Yana should start an employment agency rather than wasting her time with modeling!

I thanked him, asking myself if I hadn't seen him somewhere before. Every time I caught a glimpse of him, this feeling that I had seen him before increased. But before I could figure it out Yana linked her arm in his and quickly bustled him into the bedroom.

The bedroom in Yana's house is really strangely located because it opens directly onto the house's main entrance; this layout is completely different from what I am used to seeing in Beiruti residences, where the bedrooms are hidden behind solid walls in the depths of the houses. And Yana liked to leave her bedroom door wide open day and night.

She even left it open today when she went into the room with her boyfriend, something that really embarrassed (and even enraged!) me because I could easily hear everything that was happening between the two of them. Yana was flirting with her boyfriend in English, dropping in "habibi" and "hayati," "my darling" and "my life," after every other word. She had learned these two words after hearing them repeated constantly in the Lebanese songs she was always listening to, making them easy for her to memorize. But despite the number of times that she had heard these two words, she could not pronounce them correctly. Her native Romanian does not have the sound of the Arabic letter "h," making it impossible for her to pronounce it. Therefore, she always substituted it with "kh," a sound common to the two languages, and thus called her boyfriend "khabibi" and "khayati."

When I heard her, I thought that this small error in pronunciation could at times make a dreadful difference in meaning and lead to embarrassing results.

Yana doesn't know how to pronounce the word "hurra," for example, and this is one of the words that she uses all the time. Whenever she doesn't want to answer a question, she says, "Ana hurra, I am free!" But given that she pronounces the "ha" as "kha" and that she cannot pronounce the shadda to double the "r" sound, in her mouth this expression becomes "Ana khara, I am shit!"

Yana understands very well the difference in meaning between these two words—free and shit—but she hasn't been able to do anything to improve her pronunciation, however much she's tried.

I laughed when I thought about this but just as quickly stopped laughing because right then I remembered where I had seen her boyfriend before. I saw him one day when I went to a job interview in a hotel, he was entering the reception area accompanied by a woman with blonde hair and they were holding hands. I tried to remember if this was before Yana had met him or after they had already met, but I couldn't.

Meanwhile, the activities in the bedroom had started to heat up, increasing my embarrassment, so I decided to get away from that room and went to the kitchen, where I locked the door in order to isolate myself properly, like someone setting up a quarantine to be protected from the avian flu.

The kitchen was the only room in the house where the renovations were completed, and Yana had made a place in it for her caged parrot. This bird imposed his sovereignty over the place and would start cursing at anyone who crossed over the official border into his "territory"—that is to say, the stretch of space between the door, the stove, and the refrigerator. The moment that I crossed this border, he showered curses down upon me like rain... acid rain, of course! After the parrot had exhausted all of his ammunition, he grew silent and started observing my every movement, like a surveillance camera in one of Beirut's security zones.

When Yana bought the parrot, she didn't notice that all he could say were the most shocking curse words, because her knowledge of Arabic was extremely limited back then. In fact, she was really happy because she thought that she had purchased an "Arab" bird, who spoke the language fluently. When she discovered that he didn't recite poetry as she had thought but rather was a master in composing vulgar obscenities, she was really disappointed. But she got used to hearing these curses, so much so that she no longer was able to distinguish between these and other Lebanese expressions. She wasn't shocked if someone called her "sharmouta," for example, as some guy walking down Hamra Street did one day!

I can't forget this incident because it truly bothered me. I actually keep on remembering it and replaying the scene over and over again in my head, trying to understand the cause behind it.

We were walking down Hamra Street in front of a building known for renting out furnished rooms. No doubt the person who sidled up to us and cursed at

Yana thought that we were leaving that building, which everyone knows by the huge sign that covers an entire wall and actually means the opposite of what it says. Written on it in conspicuous innocence are the words: "Rooms for sale or rent, at reasonable prices!"

But this artificial innocence doesn't fool anyone. I know this because one day when I was walking from Yana's house to the university, early in the morning before the people of the neighborhood were awake, I noticed a change painted on the sign—someone had scratched out the word "rooms," and written "whores" in its place so that the sign read, "Whores for sale or rent, at reasonable prices!"

Yana must be the only person who doesn't know what goes on in that building! This is truly bizarre, since it isn't that far from her house and she passes by it several times a day. How could she not notice? No doubt she thinks that the building is just as innocent as its sign pretends! Yana tends to take things exactly as they appear, and I've tried to caution her about the danger of this: I'm always invoking a saying that means something like, "Things are seldom what they seem, skim milk masquerades as cream" or "Always acting so naive, makes you easier to deceive."

Yana never sees that it is actually skim milk cleverly hiding itself behind its guise as cream. She is so naïve that she is always shocked when even the tiniest indication of deception comes to light. On that day, for instance, she had a shock after informing her boyfriend that she was most likely pregnant. After he left the house, she came into the kitchen with the signs of stupefaction still on her face. She flung herself onto me, wailing, "He doesn't want to see me anymore!"… and then burst into tears.

"Shut up, sharmouta!" the parrot told her.

But Yana didn't shut up; in fact her wailing increased violently and she kept on like that for a long time. After she had finally calmed down, she apprised me in detail about everything that had happened between her and her boyfriend.

Her boyfriend was direct and clear. He gave her only two choices, no more: either she gets rid of the baby right away—if she wants to continue their relationship—or she keeps it and he's out of her life completely!

Her boyfriend put these two options before her and told her that she had to make the decision that's right for her so that she could arrive at the outcome she desires. But he cautioned her about the importance of thinking this over fully and carefully, weighing all the issues before making her final decision, because he, for his part, would not change his mind no matter what! Yana tried to make him reconsider but her efforts were fruitless.

"Case closed!" he told her. He then said, "Full stop!" and left the apartment.

After Yana had calmed down a little, she said that she didn't believe a word of it—despite how rigid he was—and that she was sure he would change his mind sooner or later! She then added, with an affected gesture, lifting her finger in the air, "He'll come crawling back to me! It's merely a question of time, that's all!"

"Shut up, sharmouta!" the parrot told her.

As for me, I said that I had to go back home because it had gotten late. But the moment I left her apartment I regretted it because I hadn't told her about having seen her boyfriend before, thereby concealing an important piece of information from her! I promised myself that I'd tell her the next day, for sure, as soon as her appointment with the gynecologist was over.

But despite this I couldn't relax, I kept thinking about it all night long and I didn't fall asleep until it was nearly dawn and I had already heard the morning azaan.

A phone call from Yasmine woke me up after only a few hours of sleep. She told me that she would come and pick me up by car in a half hour, no more. She told me to get myself ready quickly—not to waste time like I usually do—because if I wasn't ready when she got there, we'd be late for our doctor's appointment.

"Our appointment?" I wanted to say, "It's Yana's appointment and hers alone!"

But she hung up before I could say anything, without even saying goodbye.

"A waste of time" is what Yasmine considers my long periods of standing in front of the mirror, examining myself—I do this every morning, as soon as I get out of bed. I am drawn to mirrors as metal is drawn to a magnet. The mirror is the most important thing in my room and I've hung it on the wall exactly opposite the window, thinking that then the mirror could reflect the world outside my window to me.

This outside world was no longer sea and sky, as it used to be, but one morning had been transformed into a gigantic billboard, rising up on the street facing our building and blocking my view. For years, this billboard had displayed nothing but Coca-Cola ads, so that every time I looked at my likeness in the mirror, a huge bottle of Coca-Cola—with its long neck, full chest, and high waistline—was reflected behind me.

Approximately every two months, a new advertisement appears on this billboard, but the last one—in which Yana herself appears—has not changed for about six months, because it has been such a huge success. I've seen Yana's picture reflected in my mirror, behind my own reflection, every day for half of an entire year. Every day I see Yana standing next to a giant bottle of Coke and drinking from the smaller bottle she's holding. She's embracing the front of the bottle with her full, open lips, which are stained a vivid shade of red, her eyes closed, completely absorbed in what she is doing—as though drinking Coca-Cola were a divine pleasure, something completely separate from the concerns of this world.

At the bottom of the sign, giant letters spell out: *Always Coca-Cola*!

Today I also looked carefully at Yana's picture reflected behind my own likeness, because the mirror beckoned to me, pulling me toward it. That beckoning was far more powerful than Yasmine's directives about the need to hurry. Yana, as usual, was completely naked except for a red bikini, and I was facing her in my underwear.

As usual, I started inspecting my body, searching for flaws. I grabbed my breasts and pressed them close to each other and then I sucked in my belly and stood on my tiptoes to seem taller. Then I stood flat on my feet, turning around to see my rear end, which seemed really big to me, much bigger than I had hoped.

Disaster!

But the biggest disaster is the cellulite stuffed in it, which is hard for me to get rid of and gives the surface of my ass "orange-peel skin"! (This is what women's magazines call skin that has cellulite, because cellulite causes zigzags on your skin that look like an orange peel.)

Despite my love of oranges, I have always hoped that my rear end would be as smooth as two firm apples, but I know very well that I won't just wake up one morning to find it taut and tiny—voilà, it's that simple, a free gift, gratis. Only effort and exertion, and then more effort and exertion, will make this happen! Fashion models' asses have become mature fruit, only as a result of the enormous efforts that they put into them. If I want mine to look like theirs, I must work and work and work! I had adapted the exercises advised by the magazines to help smooth the skin of my two big oranges and I do them from time to time, when I feel that my bottom has started to exceed a reasonable girth.

So I squeezed my butt muscles until the two cheeks came together, as though I were holding a coin in between them and couldn't let it fall. I took a deep breath and held it in my chest, keeping it in until I almost suffocated, then I relaxed the muscles of my bottom and the imaginary coin fell out from between its cheeks.

I repeated that same exercise until my rear end started cramping from so much squeezing and began to hurt; I considered this pain a good sign of the progress that I was making to realize my goal, because Yana always says to me in French: "*Il faut souffrir pour être belle!*"

Yana doesn't have cellulite.

Yes, Yana has no cellulite. Her body is one hundred percent cellulite-free!

But her immunity to it won't last long if she really is pregnant, because her body will swell up like a ripe watermelon and cellulite will strike her with the speed of a rocket. Even worse than this, though, is that it won't be a temporary affliction, but the cellulite will cling to her rear end, hips, and thighs for a long time after she gives birth. Her beauty will be sucked out of her, as weeds suck up the rose's share of water and nourishment, so that it wilts and its fragrance dissipates. Yana's fragrance will dissipate and even vanish; it will become merely a fantasy from the past, which this surprise pregnancy will have put an end to! (Shame!)

Suddenly, I noticed that I'd wasted a lot of time looking in the mirror and that at any moment Yasmine would arrive and find me still in my underwear. This would make her crazy, because she hates to be late as much as she hates waiting; she won't wait while I choose the right clothes and get dressed, she'll drag me behind her to the clinic by my hair, as naked as I was the day God created me!

Actually, Yasmine did get really angry when she arrived, accompanied by Yana. After bursting into my room, she pointed at my underwear and said, "Is this what you've decided to go out in?" I didn't answer and so she added even more angrily, "We have to get going right now!"

This anger propelled me to put my clothes on with a speed I had never previously experienced. After I finished, we left the house, got into Yasmine's car and set off.

But our speedy exit was impeded soon after because we got stuck in a suffocating traffic jam on the Mazraa Corniche, where there was a huge amount of construction. This construction had divided the road into two sections: one part was transformed into a long ditch, which the construction workers were assiduously digging, the second part had remained intact and was reserved for the flow of traffic, but it was only wide enough for one car at a time. So one long queue of cars was lined up all the way down the road and advancing forward extremely slowly.

We entered this traffic jam because it was impossible to escape—all of the exits branching off of the main road were blocked by the construction, which had transformed the area into something of a desert, despite it being one of Beirut's busiest streets. This is because the dreadfully dense clouds of dust kept increasing, almost completely obscuring our view, so that I felt as if we were all alone in the middle of a huge dust storm.

In order to insulate ourselves from the dust, we were forced to close the windows, but this only made matters worse because the heat of the sun turned the car into an oven in which we were basically roasting like chickens. There was nothing to deliver us from this destiny because the car had no air conditioning. Despite this, we kept the windows closed because we preferred death by heat to death by choking on construction dust. This heat only increased with time so that I felt that I was no longer sitting in a seat but rather on a volcano about to erupt. In order to prevent this eruption, I tried to cool off my overheated body and reduce the inferno around me by undoing a button on my shirt, exposing a tiny bit of my chest.

At that very same moment, a group of young men mounted atop motorbikes passed close by us, moving through the tight spaces between the stopped cars like knights on horseback. One of them spotted us, broke off from his companions and stopped next to us, right on the side where I was sitting, pressing his face up against the window to stare at my unbuttoned shirt.

Then he shook his head, saying to me loudly,

"Horse!"

Yasmine immediately opened her window and said, "Donkey!" Then she laughed, which made him mad. He went over to her, reaching as if to open her car door. But she was way ahead of him and opened the door herself, pushing it against him with all her strength, making him fall off of his motorbike, the door still open. He stood up, got back on his motorbike and rode away, disappearing into the dust. Basking in our admiration, Yasmine shut the car door saying, "He thinks that he can do whatever he pleases!"

She changed the subject and said, "If only we were riding on motorbikes like him, we wouldn't have been late for our appointment!"

Next, she started enumerating the virtues of motorbikes as though she were promoting them in a commercial.

She said that they guarantee their drivers complete freedom of movement, especially on the streets of Beirut, which are always full of traffic jams. They also can get through anywhere, even narrow side streets and one-way streets, and they don't consume much gas. In addition to this, on a motorbike you can also park anywhere on the side of the road, you don't have to search for a parking spot as you do in a car. Then she said, "Enough! I've decided to replace my car with a motorbike!"

But Yasmine's desire to leave the traffic behind made her forget one extremely important thing—that she is a young woman and young women do not ride motorbikes. I reminded her of this, adding, "Wake up and snap out of it, you've got to be dreaming!"

Yasmine didn't snap out of it, though, and instead insisted that she wanted to buy a motorbike. As for me, I secretly wished that I had the courage to do something like that, because we were trapped within the sealed-up windows of this car like sardines. After a bit, when the traffic had completely stopped moving, Yasmine honked the horn violently and kept leaning on it until one of the other drivers shouted at her to stop, which she did.

With this, Yana turned on the radio—perhaps to make the time pass more quickly—and it exploded with a recently re-released song by Sabah, performed with a young singer on the cusp of fame. Yana liked this song a lot because it started, "Yana, yana, yana, yana…. I'd die for habibi."

The first time she heard this opening line, she'd thought that it was a repetition of her name and was so happy! She said, "This song is the best evidence that my name is authentically Arabic!"

Yasmine responded that the expression "yana" that Sabah was singing was not a name but rather a word that the composer used to complete the song's meter, but this didn't make much of an impression on Yana, who kept on listening to the song with pretty much the same pleasure and joy.

The person who was really saddened that Sabah's song had been re-released was my father, who told me that he had listened to the original song back in his heyday! He shook his head, adding with sorrow, "Oh, they're lost in a haze, the olden days!"

He was remembering those halcyon times, the years of his youth and glory, which coincided, at least in part, with the years of Sabah's youth and artistic glory. He sighed again and said, "Back then who would have expected that so much magnificence would simply fall apart, as if it were nothing, just to become some debris tossed back and forth in the winds of time? Who could have imagined that the Songbird would declare bankruptcy and find no other way to pay her debts than to re-record her old songs, sung together with a 'new' artist whose voice is nothing like Sabah's—no more than kenafeh tastes like a hamburger!"

He then added that this young singer's voice doesn't emanate from her mouth, but her belly button! This last comment was a clear allusion to the phenomenon of singers willing to undress for success, which always really bothers my father, and many others as well.

His comment reminded me of a joke that I once heard about Sabah—that she's had so many facelifts to make her skin wrinkle free that now her belly button also almost touches her mouth! When I told my father this joke, he didn't laugh or even smile. Scowling at me, he said, "This generation, they don't even marvel at marvels!"

Sabah's wrinkles, or more precisely, her lack of wrinkles for someone her age, is one of the reasons

Yana marvels at her. She considers Sabah, who of course she calls "Sabakh," her ideal in this respect. She hopes that she will be able to preserve her own beauty as this singer has preserved hers and to look in as good condition when she reaches the same age. Today Yana repeated this to us again, saying, "I hope that I can preserve myself like she has!"

I replied, "Preserve yourself? Do you think that you're some kind of canned good?" Yana didn't respond and actually went silent for a bit. Then she changed the radio station to one that was playing a really popular song in English, which starts like this:

This is not Paris…
This is not London…
This is not New York…
This is… Beirut!

I said, "This song could become the new Lebanese national anthem!"

But Yana didn't get the joke and as for Yasmine, she was pissed off and immediately turned off the radio, with an excess of nervous anger. Yana thanked her, saying she could feel a powerful headache coming on. Her pain persisted for the whole journey and lingered even after we had arrived in Achrafiyé and gone into the doctor's office. We were an hour late for the appointment. But the secretary who greeted us didn't comment on our lateness and just asked us to have a seat in the waiting room until the doctor was free to see us. "Go ahead, sit down and relax," she said.

But relaxing was not my concern when I entered the waiting room. I was afraid that one of the women in there would know me. I didn't relax even after I had verified that I didn't recognize even one face, in fact I was intent on making it perfectly clear to all concerned—and unconcerned—parties that I had no personal connection to this clinic whatsoever, and that I was here because I was accompanying my girlfriend to her appointment. That's it. Nothing else. In order to exculpate myself completely from any possible suspicions, I asked Yana in a voice loud enough for everyone in the room to hear, "Do you feel any better?"

But no one showed the least interest in either her or me; they were all absorbed in conversations with each other or engrossed in the magazines they were reading. Yana herself also picked up one of the magazines lying on the table in front of us, but just as quickly stopped reading it because all it contained was information about how to treat sterility and increase a woman's fertility and chances of getting pregnant. She put it back, whispering to me with open annoyance, "It's like these articles are mocking me, the woman who got pregnant by accident!"

Following up on this, I asked her if she'd changed her mind about keeping the baby, but she didn't answer. Yasmine reminded her that her pregnancy was still only a possibility, of which she still wasn't even sure. But that possibility turned into a reality when Yana went into the examination room, and after her exam the doctor announced, "Congratulations, Madame, you are in the second month of your pregnancy!"

He then added that she would give birth in seven months and about three or four weeks. Hesitantly, she asked him, "And if I decided not to give birth?" But the doctor explained to her that this would be dangerous and could lead to complications that might prevent her from getting pregnant again later.

So we left the clinic with two pieces of information: Yana's pregnancy was definite and an abortion was impossible. Yasmine proposed that we could go to another doctor who might have a different opinion. But Yana replied, "I don't want to go anywhere. Take me home."

Yasmine deferred to her wishes and when we arrived at the Starbucks building, Yana got out of the car, refusing our offer to come up to her apartment with her, saying that she could manage this on her own. She added that she really needed to soul search and think deeply about a lot of things, so we left her to do as she wished. After Yana departed, I asked Yasmine to drop me off at my grandmother's house in the Tallet al-Khayyat area, where the whole extended family was getting together for lunch as we always do after the prayers end on Friday.

The Friday prayers had already begun when we arrived at the entrance to the building where my grandmother lived and the nearby mosque's loudspeakers were broadcasting the khutba for everyone to hear. I guessed that "American hegemony" was the topic of this sermon because the person delivering it repeated that expression over and over as I climbed the stairs to the fifth floor. It took me a long time to climb up the never-ending stairs—I felt as if I was climbing all the way up to the heavens and not just to my grandmother's house. I silently cursed the electricity company that had decided to cut the current to this neighborhood the moment I arrived so that I couldn't take the elevator.

When I finally reached the landing in front of the apartment I was panting from exhaustion and my shirt was damp under the arms with perspiration, producing an odor like a fishmonger's shop at noon. I planned to wash as soon as I entered the house, but the women sitting on the living room floor detained me. I had to shake their hands, each woman one by one, and kiss each one three times on her cheeks, then ask each one about her health—even though I knew that the health of every single one of them was good and nothing was wrong with any of them! This process of delivering greetings lasted a long time because, as usual, there were a large number of women present. They successfully exploited their numbers to increase the productivity and speed of lunch preparation and had divided the discrete tasks involved amongst themselves.

This process was now reaching its climax: my mother Hiba and my grandmother Naziha were preparing balls of kibbeh, and my father's sister Nahid and her three daughters were chopping tomatoes and parsley, and my father's other, recently engaged, sister Nuha was peeling onions and crying because they were so strong, and my father's third sister Niemat and her two daughters Zaynab and Hala were peeling potatoes, which my father's brother's wife Hanadi cut up to fry in oil later. As for Dareen, the wife of my father's other brother, and her daughter Ulaa, the two of them were drinking coffee with Ru'aa, the fiancée of my father's third brother, and also with my grandmother's neighbor Siham, and her son's wife, whose name I tried to remember but couldn't.

These women had brought their children along to my grandmother's house, just as they do every Friday, and the number of kids in the apartment was approximately the same as the number of inhabitants in a small village.

Today this village was packed into a three-room apartment—it has an entry hall, a living room, and a bedroom. The population density had reached a level that would shock the United Nations bureau responsible for the world's overpopulation problem. But the overcrowded numbers of children wasn't the worst of it—the worst was the roar emanating from them, loud enough to wake the Companions of the Cave from their deep slumber. Despite their desperate mothers' attempts to calm them, the children were jumping and screaming and running through the house without stopping or tiring. It was as though inside them they had limitless energy, exactly like the Duracell battery that keeps on going and going and going...

This roar had gone on for much longer than the mothers could stand, their anger toward their children exploded and was incarnated in my uncle's wife Hanadi, who got up from the floor where she was sitting to impose some order. She found that she could only conquer by dividing and so she split the kids into two groups. She sent the first to the shop on the ground floor of the building owned by my grandmother's elderly neighbor, telling her oldest son, whom she appointed as the group's leader, to buy her sanitary pads, "Buy some Always!"

"Always?" I asked her curiously, after the first detachment of children had marched off to execute her order.

She replied that she's embarrassed to buy them herself from the mini-market near her house because she's too shy to speak of such intimate things in front of the three young men who work there. So she prefers to buy them from an old man, like the one who owns the shop on the ground floor of my grandmother's building. I reminded her that it's not she who'll feel embarrassed in either place anyway, because her son's the one who's buying the pads for her. But Hanadi didn't hear me because she was busy with the second group of children; she had ordered them to sit in a row on the sofa and keep silent—under threat of getting smacked with a slipper that she had taken off and waved right in their faces to assure them that she wasn't joking.

And just like that, the noise died down; I could no longer hear anything but the women's chatting, the loudspeaker on the minaret of the nearby mosque and the sound of the television, which was broadcasting a song called "Tannoura" (Oh, Why Does She Shorten her Skirt?). But my grandmother wasted no time in turning off the song after the azaan started, causing a group mobilization of the women sitting in the living room, who instantly suspended their activities and headed all together to the apartment's one sink to do their wudu'.

Now I myself had intended to head toward the very same sink just seconds before the azaan started so that I could wash my armpits and get rid of the smell of rotting fish radiating from them. But I didn't get there in time for two reasons: firstly, as soon as the women heard the azaan they rushed to the sink like cars speeding down the highway, cutting me off with blows from their hips and elbows, practically crushing me; secondly, at that moment, my cousin Hala grabbed my right arm and dragged me away into the bedroom.

In the bedroom, she told me in a whisper, "Abeer, I don't want to get married!"

Stupefied, I asked her, "What did you say?" For it had really shocked me—in fact it shocked me a great deal more than it should have—I felt as if she was saying to me, "Abeer, I'm actually a man!"

Even though she hadn't given her reasons for her lack of desire to marry, I immediately connected her statement to a possible confusion about her sexual orientation—something that I had wondered about for a long time, without ever openly saying anything to her. My evidence for this was her long-standing refusal to get married.

This refusal has really infuriated her family, but for a different reason—Hala had already reached thirty years of age and thus was only a few steps away from the point of no return from the hell they call spinsterhood. This caused her mother acute pain and embarrassment and everyone took part in adding to this pain and this embarrassment, first and foremost my aunt Nahid, who had married off all her daughters a long time ago and who always says to Hala's mother, "Isn't it a shame that this flower will wilt before anyone's inhaled its fragrance?"

Though this flower—i.e., Hala—really had begun to wilt, that doesn't mean that no one has desired to breathe in her fragrant scent, for potential grooms have been flocking to her family's house in droves from the time she reached a marriageable age—they sought her out as if they were flies and she the blue light that would zap them. But Hala's response was always the same, even as time kept passing. To every single one of them, she would very simply say two words, never three:

"Ma baddi!" (meaning: No!)

She would pronounce these two words, lifting the palm of her right hand in the air and turning her face to the side to emphasize what she had just said, as though she were one of the princesses in the stories of *1001 Nights*, who won't consent to marry unless it is to a man who truly deserves her. Now the man who truly deserves her is the strongest in all the land: he's always prepared to go to the ends of the earth for her sake, to launch wars against all the other kingdoms and make the grandest of their leaders bow down at his feet as confirmation of both his absolute power and his everlasting love for her.

But none of these potential bridegrooms confirmed his everlasting love for Hala or launched a war, even a small one, for her sake, not one of them even protested against her rejecting him or got down on his knees to beg her to reconsider, as she would have liked in her dreams. And so she was left disappointed every time, but she wasn't too sad about it; in her opinion these disappointing men weren't worthy of her anyway, since they weren't ever real men. For her, this was the root of the problem—she always used to claim that the reason she refused to get married was her search for this "real man" and her dissatisfaction with anything less!

Tracking him down is no simple matter. He'd be a rare find, because this is an endangered species! His kind is on the brink of extinction.

This is what Hala always used to tell me, without providing any detailed information about this breed, or the criteria that she used to distinguish "real" men from other men—the only thing that I knew about real men is that they didn't cross her path.

But as circumstances would have it, when she was

thirty years old, a man of this rare breed finally did cross her path and asked for her hand in marriage. And she refused. And he insisted, so she accepted. The wedding planning came on like a sudden torrential downpour in the most arid desert after a drought that has lasted for years, when everything that's wilted suddenly comes alive. Hala herself came alive in the eyes of her aunts and uncles on both her mother's and father's sides, and to the rest of the extended family, too. To them she had become a flower blooming at the peak of its maturity, a prize blossom to be plucked, smelled, and enjoyed.

So this flower finally surrendered her hand in marriage to her knight in shining armor, who came to her riding atop a rented white 2007 Cadillac, in place of a white horse. According to Hala, this knight, whose name happens to be Faris (meaning knight in Arabic), he is everything that she had dreamed of and desired—and more.

"So what's the problem, then?" I asked her.

"The problem…" Hala began, but was silenced just as quickly by my grandmother coming into the bedroom to do her noontime prayers.

My grandmother's entrance at that moment was the commercial break that interrupts a film on television, giving the viewers a chance to move away from the screen for a moment without missing anything. Her intrusion let me escape from Hala and her story for a second and go to the bathroom to escape from my sweaty shirt.

After I had traded my shirt for house clothes and put on some perfume, I returned to the bedroom, where my grandmother had already finished her prayers. But she didn't leave the room as I expected and instead started organizing one of her wardrobes, though all of them are always perfectly organized. Her sudden organizational frenzy prevented us from continuing our conversation, which annoyed Hala, who wanted to talk so much that she was on the verge of exploding. When she could repress this urge no longer, she grabbed me by the arm and dragged me to one of the corners of the room, saying very loudly, "How long have you gone without plucking your eyebrows? The hair on them is almost as thick as the shrubbery in Sanayeh Park!"

I was about to say that the shrubbery in that park could hardly be called thick and that the few shrubs growing there could be counted on one person's fingers and toes. But I resisted because I noticed that Hala wasn't listening to me and had started searching for the eyebrow tweezers. After she found them in a drawer, she came right up close to me and started plucking the grass growing in this "garden" out by its roots. She used this as a pretext to whisper into my ear the story of how her wedding plans were failing without arousing our grandmother's suspicion—grandma would try to figure out what we were talking about straightaway if she realized that we were hiding something important from her.

This actually was something important, or the

tone of Hala's voice at least made it seem like it was. She brought her face so close to mine that our lips were almost touching and I could feel the warmth of her breath on me, as she whispered, "That low-life despicable man! Thank God I found out what he's really like before the wedding!"

She then explained that Faris wasn't actually the knight in shining armor that she thought she had found. In fact, she had only found a poseur knight and she had discovered this pose exactly two days before, when they were hanging out together in one of the bars in Gemmayzeh. Late that night, two men who were clearly drunk came over to their table. One of them started to curse at her fiancé for no reason. The other came up to Hala and tried to put his hand on her breasts. Instead of getting the man off her, as she expected him to do and he should have done, Faris bent his head so that it was almost hidden underneath the table and not a single sound crossed his lips except the chattering of his teeth.

"He was afraid!" Hala whispered to me, shaking her head. She added, in serious distress, "He turned out to be a *tante* in the end! A sissy! A fag!"

She then plucked a bunch of little hairs from my right eyebrow in one violent motion as though taking revenge on the universe that had sent her a fag fiancé, and I shouted out in pain.

At that moment, my mother came into the bedroom to tell us that she had seen the men returning from the mosque and that we should prepare some coffee for them. Hala took on this task and so I went to open the door for my father, brothers, Uncle Khalid, Uncle Ahmad, and his son, who had not yet entered the house but were standing outside waiting for the end of the hijab-putting-on-process in the living room. This hijab-putting-on-process at first glance seems simple and easy, but it actually involves a complicated computational process: every woman must calculate her relative relationship with each one of the men, and as quickly as possible, to deduce whether she must put on a hijab to hide her charms from him, even if she has no charms.

The women used their tried and true expertise to finish these calculations with the speed of a new computer. As they covered their hair, they looked to me like women warriors putting on their helmets to prepare for a battle that they might have to rush into at any second. When they were at last ready for this battle, the men came into the living room, greeted the women and then evicted the children from the sofas, occupying them themselves.

These sofas, however, didn't have enough room for all of them and my cousin Muhammad was left standing because he hadn't entered the living room with the first wave. When I walked over to say hello and shake his hand as I usually do, he took a quick step backwards and put his hand on his heart, preventing me from shaking it. This really surprised me—he'd shaken my hand no problem only one week before. Could such a change happen in just one week?

In accordance with this sudden, peculiar change, my cousin maintained, at minimum, an arm's length distance from me, until the whole family gathered around the lunch table. This table was barely big enough for all of us, in our large numbers, so we were jammed in around it like bodies on Judgment Day. It was so tight around the table that my cousin was obliged to get very close to me and his thigh touched mine under the table; our thighs remained stuck together throughout the whole lunch. He didn't try to move away and neither did I—on purpose.

After everyone had finished their food, my Uncle Khalid asked me, while pouring himself a glass of Coca-Cola, "How's your friend Yana? Is she still sick?"

I knew instantly that the news of Yana's alleged illness had reached him by way of Hala's long, wagging tongue, and thus that everyone at the table had also received it. Now they all insisted on knowing what was afflicting Yana, because they all were eagerly anticipating her presence at the wedding, and mercilessly they pressed me with the same question, over and over, "What's wrong with her?"

"Nothing!" I answered after a few moments of confusion, in a tone that was more a call for help than anything else.

I was actually calling for help, but to a divine power, to intervene at that moment and help me face them. But my family kept on insisting and I felt betrayed! Betrayed by this power that I had called upon but that didn't respond. I felt the kibbeh that I had eaten suddenly turn into a pile of rocks sitting heavily in my stomach, making me feel as though I had to vomit. How could I not vomit: the mere thought of them knowing about Yana's pregnancy gave me stomach cramps! If they knew, it would mean only shame and disgrace!

Yes, shame and disgrace! What would they think of me, since I'm her friend? What would my father think, for example? He's the one who always repeats that Arabic proverb, "If you grow close to a group of people, after 40 days you become one of them!" He would definitely think that I had become exactly like Yana in every way and that because Yana is having extramarital relations with some man, I must be as well, after all, am I not someone who's grown close to her? And my closeness to her has lasted far longer than 40 days!

So as not to transform into the living embodiment of this proverb in everyone's eyes, I decided to protect myself and make them believe that my relationship with Yana was over.

"It's over," I said in English. "I ended my relationship with her," I added with feigned severity, hoping that they wouldn't notice my lack of acting ability and would totally believe that what I was saying was the truth.

So that no one would discover that I had lied, I called Yana as soon as I got back home and asked her not to say anything about her pregnancy to Hala. I also asked her never to call me on my home phone, on the pretext that the telephone in my bedroom was broken and so there was only one phone left in the house, which was in the living room, where my family always sits and listens when anyone talks on the telephone—especially when the electricity's been cut and they can't watch television.

Yana believed what I told her and assured me that she would only call me on my mobile. Then she added, "In any case, I won't be calling you much in the coming two days, because I want to go into seclusion and think for a long time!"

"Think about what? About existence?" I said to her. She replied, "Yes! Existence!" I wanted to ask her if she thought that becoming an ascetic in an apartment above Starbucks would allow her to encounter the truth more directly, but I demurred. Yana said that she'd call me once a day the following week, after I had started working at the Coca-Cola Company, so that I could supply her with daily strength by giving her news of her boyfriend.

"I'm assigning you to spy on him!" she told me jokingly.

But to Yana's bad luck, spying was not one of my better skills: I returned to her empty-handed after finishing my first day of work at the company. My aptitude for spying did not improve even after five days of trying, and her boyfriend's way of dealing with me contributed to my failure. He kept every conversation with me short and limited to work-related things: he would ask and I would execute—without additions, amendments, or any extra commentary.

Despite this, Yana insisted on asking me every day if I could figure anything out about him or their relationship from his behavior, looks, or words. Every day I would answer her, with increasing irritation:

"No!"

When she called me one morning about a week after I'd started the job, she surprised me by not mentioning her boyfriend and saying, "I've thought a lot about my pregnancy and I've arrived at the right decision!"

Finally, I said to myself, the truth has revealed itself to Yana! But when I asked her to enlighten me about this truth, she refused. Her refusal was unequivocal. She said that she couldn't tell me an important thing like this over the phone and we agreed to meet that very afternoon, right after I finished my classes at the university, so that she could tell me in person. Our meeting time coincided with her appointment at the beauty salon, so I would meet her at her place and go with her to her appointment.

After we agreed on this, I hung up and stood in front of the mirror, as I do every morning. The picture from the Coca-Cola advertisement was reflected in it as always. But today the picture didn't look how I was used to seeing it: Yana's always naked body was now hidden beneath a thick coat of black paint—no part of her body was showing except her face and her shoulders.

No doubt this transformation had happened at

night and the person who covered Yana with paint did his deed while everyone was sleeping. The result of this action was that today Yana looked like she was wearing a black abaya, like the ones Bedouin women wrap around themselves in films! As for her black hair, it covered her head as though it were a hijab, and seemed to extend all the way down to the abaya. This new look was so strange on her it really made me laugh. The hijab and Yana would never meet—even if the heavens crashed down onto earth or the opposite, if the earth rose up to touch the heavens! I told Yasmine this when she came to see me that same day, but she didn't find it funny, quite the opposite in fact, because what had happened to the ad saddened her. She said, "It looks like she's wearing mourning clothes!" and then after a few seconds had passed she added, "Well, that's fitting for the occasion!"

I asked her, "What occasion?" noticing that she herself was also wearing black. "Who died?" I asked. She answered, "My neighbor, Waleed."

She said it very simply, as though to her it was self-evident, indeed as though she had been expecting it to happen for a while. When I asked her how he died, she said that she didn't know but his family claimed that he had died the evening before of a sudden attack of angina, though she didn't believe them, because Waleed had been absent from his usual spot at the building's entrance for almost a week now.

"Strange," Yasmine said finally, and sighed.

But I didn't see anything strange in this, the man (that is if he was in fact a man) had died, he simply died, everyone dies—full stop, case closed. But Yasmine didn't consider the case closed, and instead asked me to accompany her to the funeral so that together we could find out what happened. I declined with the excuse that I had to go to the university right away.

When I arrived at the university, I found my friends in their usual gathering place, all listening intently to Ashraf and not noticing me as I approached. Ashraf was telling a joke that he never tired of repeating because he thought it was so funny. He always performed it in a really dramatic way, without leaving anything out or adding a single word. Despite the stability of the joke's text, he added a lot of interpretation to its performance: he changed the tone of his voice to suit the characters and increased his pace when he wanted to achieve more dramatic impact. This performance of his would practically have been like the full staging of a play had the joke he was telling not been so trite.

Here's the joke:

A lady goes into a greengrocer's shop, rushes right to the box of cucumbers and starts examining its contents, one cucumber after another, touching each one of them carefully. After she finishes, she asks the grocer how much a kilo costs, and he answers her laughing, "1000LL for a kilo... Madame!" Completely shocked, the woman changes color and freezes in her spot, unable to speak! After she recovers from her shock, her color returns to normal and once she can speak again, she says, "But how… how do you know that I am Madame and not Mademoiselle?" The greengrocer laughs again and adds, "Seriously, Madame? From the way you handle the cucumbers!"

Here, Ashraf stops his narration suddenly and the crowd gathered around him bursts out laughing. There is no doubt that Ashraf takes this laughter as the closest possible thing to warm applause because it always seems to me as if he's about to bow, exactly as actors do after a successful performance.

Today as well, the group burst out laughing and after they had calmed down I said to Ashraf, "We're in the twenty-first century and you're still telling jokes about who's a 'Madame'?! Do you think that you're living in a tent in the desert?"

He replied, "Listen to me, Abeer! I love you like a sister, so I'm going to tell you this: Don't let the winds lead you astray! Don't let them lead you to hell!" When I asked him what he meant, and exactly which winds he was referring to, as there are many kinds of winds that blow in Lebanon—they come and go depending on the season and the weather—he lifted an angry finger in the air and told me, "The winds that make you stray from the straight path."

After a silence of a few seconds, he added, "A girl is like a flower, she can only be plucked once! Once she's been plucked, she wilts and her fragrance disappears." He also added, "Actually, she's like a bottle of

Coke, it can only be opened once! Who would buy a bottle of Coke that's already been opened?" He thought a bit and added further, "Actually, a girl is like a tall glass of lemonade!"

But I didn't even get what he was driving at with this example and asked him to clarify, so he told me that a glass of lemonade is made up of three ingredients: lemons, water, and sugar. You can't do away with any one of them because the absence of one prevents you from making the lemonade. Similarly, a young woman isn't complete unless three attributes are found in her, and you can't do away with any one of these either! She must be a virgin, a wife, and a mother—in that order, of course! If a young woman doesn't possess the combination of these three attributes or if her upbringing is somehow faulty, she'll immediately—with no indecision, doubt, or delay—become the "Madame" about whom hundreds of jokes are told.

"Am I clear?" Ashraf sealed off his speech, his tone that of a good Muslim who's trying to guide one of the lost Ahl al-dhimma back to God's straight path. His tone really frightened me—it was as if he had doubts about my virginity! I was afraid that these doubts might have also run through the minds of all the people there because they heard our conversation and I wanted to say to them: Don't misunderstand me! I'm not at all what you think! In fact, I am 100% virgin, 100% pure, 100% chaste… with no additives! And with a lot, really a lot, of preservatives!

But I didn't say anything. I was aware that mere words could convert their suspicions into the truth. So I decided to laugh in response to Ashraf because laughter indicates confidence and might conceal my embarrassment.

Then I looked at my watch and noticed that it was already time for my class, so I quickly said good-bye to everyone and left. After I attended all of my classes, I left the university and headed for Yana's apartment. The second she opened the door she said, "We have to rush so that we're not late."

We hurried off to the Hawwa' Beauty Salon, which Yana called "Khawwa'," and which was frequented by a lot of her fashion model friends. This salon was on the main street in Verdun, not far from Yana's house—only about a quarter of an hour walking distance at the very most. Despite this, today we set off a full hour before the appointment because Yana couldn't walk at a normal pace in her high heels, which were practically a part of her feet since she only took them off when sleeping. Even at this incredibly slow place, walking was still the quickest way to reach the salon because the many checkpoints in the area cause traffic jams. The security situation requires the police to examine the registration of passing cars periodically and also to check all the passengers' identity cards. This creates clogged-up bottlenecks on most Beirut streets; traffic can be stopped for long hours and walking is the only way to escape this fate.

Nevertheless, I hate walking on Beirut's streets because its lack of proper sidewalks makes me feel that using them for transportation is a truly life-threatening adventure; motorbikes and even cars for that matter whiz past me as though they were trying to assassinate me but changed their mind at the very last minute. I especially hate walking when I'm with Yana because she attracts everyone's attention—everybody stares at her as if they were Bedouins faced with a lush oasis and they look away from me completely as if I were nothing, merely a mirage.

Today as usual, I felt like nothing, just a mirage, and as usual I was annoyed. Yana asked me what was wrong. Trying to change the subject, I said, "So why don't you tell me what decision you've arrived at after all your pious seclusion?"

She responded that she had made two decisions: The first is that she had settled on the child's name, after really having been uncertain about it. So I asked her, "What's the name?" And she replied, "Saree!"

She had come across it on the internet on a website devoted to the meanings and cultural and geographical origins of thousands of names. The name "Saree," according to this site, is an Arabic name meaning "night traveler." Yana immediately fell in love with it because for her it conjured up infinitely expansive valleys, moonlit sand dunes, a horseman atop his mount under a clear, star-filled sky. When she asked my opinion, I told her waveringly that it was a very pretty name. In reality, however, I didn't like it, because to me the expression "night traveler" evokes only late-night flights, which I truly hate. I find night travel very annoying and oppressive, especially because it messes up my sleep patterns.

And as for Yana's second decision, it was to remain in Lebanon permanently. This will force her to look for another job because the modeling agency refused to employ her while she's pregnant. She thought that she might have found another job yesterday at a hotel near her house. They urgently needed a young lady to greet clients and she felt after the interview that the manager had really liked her and so would choose her specifically out of all of the women who had applied for the position—he had assured her that he would call her soon.

"Did he call you?" I asked her immediately.

But he hadn't called her yet, though she expected him to call at any moment, because her intuition assured her that this would happen without a doubt. Her intuition also assured her that fate would return to her something essential that had been taken from her in the previous week… this something was her boyfriend. Because this intuition of hers had the ability to foresee coming events but not the precise time that they would happen, Yana didn't know the exact moment when her boyfriend would come back to her. Therefore, she decided to be prepared for this moment at all times and arranged with the beauticians at the Hawwa' salon to implement a rigorous beauty program so that her body would always be well-maintained and ready for anything.

When we finally arrived at the salon, I asked her which part of the program was scheduled for today and she replied, "Today I will get plucked like a chicken."

By this, she meant that she would remove all of the hair on her body with wax, to make her arms, legs, upper lip, eyebrows, underarms, and even her "private parts" smooth and silky, ready to be touched and caressed. In addition to this plucking party she was going to have her hair cut "with brushing" and also get a full spa manicure and pedicure with nail polish. From what she said, I understood that we wouldn't be leaving the salon before its scheduled closing time and before the women working there were due to finish their shift for the day. I was trying to think of a way that I could waste time while Yana was completing her beauty regimen. When one of the beauticians suggested that I also beautify myself, I realized that this was actually the most appropriate way to pass the time. I declined, however, because I didn't have enough money on me to do it. But I didn't tell Yana this, so she couldn't understand why I had refused and, surprised, asked me, "Why?"

She began inspecting my entire body as though I were a car on display for sale and then said, "You at least need to have your upper lip plucked—you've got a man's mustache! The hair on your upper lip is so thick that it's practically turned your face into an overgrown garden!"

I knew that she was saying this to make me laugh.

But I didn't laugh and instead explained to her that the reason I wasn't getting my upper lip plucked was because of a big cold sore that had appeared there two days ago, which would make removing the hair from it an extremely painful affair, indeed even torture!

But Yana was not convinced and replied, "*Il faut souffrir pour être belle!*" This expression reminded me of another expression in the same language that my cousin Hala used to repeat to me constantly, though she didn't speak French at all: "*à la perfection.*" Hala never leaves the house before everything about her appearance is arranged totally à la perfection, because she's obsessed with her own beauty. She dreams of people comparing her to a foreign movie star, because those actresses are, in her opinion, the very pinnacle of beauty, a peak that Hala always dreams of ascending!

But Hala will never reach this pinnacle no matter how hard she tries because she can't ever transform into the pale, blonde girl, with "colored" eyes that she's always dreamed of being. In order to achieve this dream she imposes relentless restrictions on her body, but it fights them just as it would a malignant disease.

Her brown hair, for example, is always thriving, pushing itself through the surface of her scalp as though it's resisting the suppression of its real color by the blonde dye with which she suffocates it. You can clearly see the brown color of her eyes behind the green-tinted contact lenses that don't completely succeed in covering her round, wide pupils. As for her skin, it returns to its original brown after only a few hours of sun exposure, even if its owner submerges it in whitening cream.

Despite this, Hala remains determined to tame her body, continually re-imposing these restrictions on it.

This is exactly what she was doing today when we met her in the beauty salon, that is to say when Yana had already begun her arduous and event-filled day with the least tedious and painful part—getting her hair blown dry and brushed out straight. To tell the truth, I was not sure why she insisted on this blowing and brushing, because her hair was naturally smooth and straight... the opposite of Hala's kinky, frizzy hair. Hala herself was also amazed when she saw what Yana was doing and said, "I'm so jealous of you! If I had hair like yours, I'd be able to brush it out straight by myself! If I only had hair like yours, I could just relax!"

But Hala couldn't just relax; her hair wouldn't let her. Hala was also surprised at the color of Yana's hair, midnight black—she walked up close to her and started inspecting it to be sure that it wasn't dyed, for Hala thought that "foreigners," as she had always imagined them, could only be blonde, the very same blonde that she used to dye her own hair.

After Hala had finished getting her hair done, she made a plan with Yana to go the following day to the tailor who was going to make Hala's wedding gown.

"What wedding?" I asked her, surprised, since I

thought that she had changed her mind about getting married! But Hala looked at me like someone who really didn't want to discuss this, then turned her back to us and left!

Yana also left, not to go outside, but to the salon's other wing in order to get her nails done and afterward remove her body hair. She left me alone to wait for her. When she returned, her white skin had turned bright red, because when hair is pulled out by its roots it temporarily leaves a mark on the skin. Yana asked me to come with her to the place where they would wax off her pubic hair and took me by the hand, saying, "Don't leave me, I'll suffer all alone!"

So I went with her to a small room in the depths of the salon, covered with thick drapes on all four sides, which reminded me of the prison torture rooms that I had seen in some film.

Inside, Yana took off her clothes and then lay down on the long bed and opened her legs exactly as she did at the gynecologist's office. I stood in front of her and held her hand. At that moment, one of the beauticians entered the room; she covered the area between Yana's legs with warm wax, then covered the wax with a special paper and started rubbing it so that the hair would stick to the wax. Then she took the edges of the paper and ripped it off of Yana's pubic area in one quick, violent motion, so that Yana screamed out in pain. She screamed and clenched her stomach and quickly closed her legs, lifting her thighs up to her chest all the while squeezing my hand hard.

When the pain had subsided somewhat, she opened her legs back up and the beautician repeated the process several more times until her pubic area was completely free of hair. Yana then loosened her grip on my hand and I noticed at that moment that both of our hands were damp with sweat.

Smiling, the beautician said to her in English, "You are smoother than silk!" Yana answered her, "And as red as a tulip in bloom!"

After all the hair had been ripped off of it, Yana's pubic area had become bright red, so that it resembled a chicken roasted on a grill more than a tulip in bloom. When I told her this, she responded that she felt as though the whole area had actually been roasted on a grill—exactly like a chicken. It was really hot and red because of the plucking, as though it had actually been lain down upon live coals. She said this then grabbed my hand, pulling it toward her, between her legs, to prove to me the truth of what she was say-ing. But I extracted my hand from her grasp with an unintended violence that pushed me backward so powerfully I almost fell.

Yana laughed and then said that we had to wait a few more minutes before leaving the salon, until the heat of her pubic area was less intense, because that heat was an indication that her pubic area was still very sensitive. This makes putting her trousers back on extremely painful and makes walking in them a torture. She had once made the mistake of putting her trousers back on quickly and felt them chafing against her pubic area while she was walking as though they were grating it.

So that Yana's pubic area wouldn't be grated again, we didn't leave the salon until she was confident that it had cooled off sufficiently. When we finally did leave, my friend stood on the edge of the traffic-filled street and said, "I'm really tired and I can't take any more! I want to go home. I hope a taxi will come right away!"

The very moment that she said this, a car with the word "taxi" in Arabic letters on an illuminated sign on its roof stopped in front of us; two women were already sitting in it. A bald, dark-skinned young man was driving it and asked us where we wanted to go, so Yana answered him in Arabic, "Khamra!" with her ha' sounding really more like a kha' as usual.

The young man burst out laughing and then said with obvious malice, "Sorry, I don't know any place in all of Lebanon called Khamra!"

Then he drove on without saying anything else.

What a jerk, I said to myself!

There's no doubt that Yana understood he was making fun of her, because under her breath, with the usual mispronounced "kh," she called him an ass, "khimar!"

She then announced that she wouldn't ride in shared taxis anymore; I pointed out that this would be really hard on her because these vehicles are her preferred method of transportation in Beirut. She doesn't have a car and hates waiting for the public buses, which don't keep to their schedules. Furthermore, these taxis are indispensable, especially in the summer when walking in the sun is a kind of masochism.

Yana wanted to respond to my little speech but my mobile phone rang, preventing her. My phone's screen showed that the caller was my boss, so before answering I moved a little away from my friend for fear that she would hear his voice. But his voice reached Yana despite the distance between us, because he started shouting the moment that I answered the phone. From the look on Yana's face, it was obvious that she had heard the shouting but had no idea who was calling. She started moving toward me to try to hear the voice coming out of the phone better, but she didn't reach me in time because the call was very short.

Her (ex-) boyfriend limited what he had to say to exactly two sentences: he told me that he had just spent an entire half hour searching for papers related to a very important business deal and couldn't find them, accusing me personally of losing them. And then he ordered me to come to the office right away and find these papers at once, or else…

Or else what? I wanted to ask him, but I couldn't because he hung up on me.

At first, I was upset, but I realized that I should react immediately, and asked Yana to go back to Hamra alone, convincing her to ride in a shared servees taxi that had a man and woman already in it.

Then I stood waiting for another servees to take me to Hazmiyeh, where the Coca-Cola Company is located, but none of the drivers who passed by agreed to take me there unless I paid the full private taxi fare because it was so far away.

I had expected this to happen because Hazmiyeh is located at a fair distance from where I was, but I hadn't taken enough money with me that day to pay the full fare for a private taxi. So there was really nothing I could do but wait—I had to convince a driver to agree to take me for the little money that I had on me. But after waiting for a full quarter of an hour with no relief from my suffering, and without any relief announcing its imminent arrival, I started to lose hope and wished that some kind of divine intervention would deliver me from this situation.

This intervention came—in the form of a young man riding on a scooter, who stopped in front of me and offered to drop me off wherever I wanted. I knew that this young man was a student at LAU because I'd often seen him there, though we'd never exchanged a word. I accepted his proposal on the condition that I could wear the helmet that was on his head. I didn't so much want to protect my head from accidents as to hide my face behind it for fear that some family member or acquaintance might see me riding on a motorbike, and with a young man they didn't know, at that!

Though he was a stranger, I accepted the ride on this young man's motorbike because firstly, he seemed trustworthy and also because it was my only way to reach the office. (And where's the shame in that?)

After I put on the helmet and made sure that it covered my face well, I tucked up the hem of my dress, sat behind him on the motorbike's leather seat and suddenly felt its heat between my open legs. I tried to sit on the edge of it to be as far as possible from the young man and not touch him, but I found this impossible, especially after we got going, as I was forced to wrap my arms around his waist, with my chest touching his back, to keep from falling off. I clutched him even tighter when we entered a traffic-filled street because our route was blocked; my fingernails almost ripped his clothes when the motorbike leaned to the right or left in narrow, twisting passageways. When we got out of the traffic and set off on the open road, I relaxed my grip on him and put my hand on my thigh to fix my dress back into place because the wind had made it flap so violently that it had almost completely ridden up my legs. I was bothered while riding because it had been extremely difficult for me to keep my balance and my legs covered at the same time.

Even though I was bothered by my skirt, I felt a surprising freedom the whole time I was on the road and I also suddenly felt energized, full of life!

This sensation had made me forget my confrontation with my boss until we arrived at the company door. The young man offered to wait for me. I thanked him, but refused, afraid I might keep him waiting for a really long time. Even though he insisted, I refused a second time—his eagerness frightened me. I turned my back and walked toward my boss's office, where he was still waiting for me.

He was still extremely angry, so much so that he started shouting right in my face the moment he saw me, but I ignored his shouting and began searching for the lost papers right away. But the fact that I ignored his shouting didn't allay his anger as I had hoped and even expected it would, in fact it did the opposite. This actually increased his anger; a few minutes later he walked over to me, ripped some papers out of my hand and threw them onto the floor. His hand touched my shoulder when he did this and I felt a slight shiver—at that moment I wished that I had listened to Yana and plucked my mustache earlier that day. I covered my upper lip with my hand to hide the protruding hairs but he came up right beside me, so close that our bodies were almost touching, and suddenly tore my hand away and kissed me violently on the mouth. I immediately pulled myself away from him, but he came toward me a second time, grabbing me by the shoulder and pushing me to the ground. He opened my legs with his knees and threw himself down on top of me. I tried to fight him off but he was really heavy, and I wished that the young man with the motorbike would come and save me. But of course he didn't come. When he entered me between my legs I didn't see anything except the edge of his shoulder and the Coca-Cola advertisement, the one Yana appeared in, hanging on the wall behind him.

After I got home, I saw the very same advertisement again out my open bedroom window and I angrily closed my curtains. I threw myself down on my bed without taking off my clothes and changing into pajamas, without even taking off my shoes. I closed my eyes and tried to sleep, but I couldn't. What surprised me was that I was thinking about Yana more than I was thinking about what had happened to me...

Only a few minutes after I got home, Yana called me on my mobile phone. The moment that I saw her name flashing on my phone's screen, I made two quick decisions: first, I wouldn't answer her call and second, I would cut off all relations with her completely and decisively. At that very moment, the moment when I made these two decisions, I felt a kind of pain between my thighs, which got increasingly severe until I couldn't bear it any longer and had to take a painkiller.

It took me a while to come to terms with this, despite its profound significance—if it weren't for the pain, I wouldn't even have noticed that I had been deflowered or that something inside me had completely changed! This surprised me; it surprised me that I didn't feel any change, I had always thought that the moment you lose your virginity is a turning point in life and that for me, of all people, everything would change at that moment... I would surely transform into another woman, in all the different meanings the word implies—in the blink of an eye, I would change from a small, closed-up bud into a blossoming flower, from a tightly spun cocoon into a brilliant butterfly!

But today I realized that flowers and butterflies or any other plants and insects have nothing to do with this, because I'm just exactly who I am—and who I was an hour or a day or two days or a month or three months before. There was no outward sign to suggest that I had been "deflowered" except the blood stains in my underwear, which really looked a lot like menstrual blood, actually exactly the same! This also surprised me because these two things are contradictory! The blood of virginity is the purest thing in my existence and is indeed the very reason for my entire existence, whereas the blood of menstruation is impurity, unclean blood that my body must rid itself of once a month. There can be no doubt or suspicion whatsoever at all about the truth of this!

But the blood in my underwear looks a lot like menstrual blood.

Thinking about menstruation reminded me that my own period has to come and that it has to come exactly when it's due without being even one day late, because I—as a result of the day's events—could be pregnant. I was really shaken up by this possibility— even if I could hide that I'd lost my virginity, I wouldn't be able to hide a swelling belly that kept getting bigger and bigger! Everyone knows that pregnancy isn't something to take lightly, especially if that pregnancy is the fruit of a relationship conducted outside of the purview of marriage. (I say the "fruit of" even though I'm not a tree.)

But Yana's pregnancy is also the fruit of an extra-marital relationship (even though Yana isn't a tree either), her relationship with her boyfriend, who wasn't married to her and didn't even plan to marry her. Despite all this, it was a simple matter for Yana: her foreign citizenship empowers her. Yana can get pregnant and give birth without thinking of getting married—not for a second or even a fraction of a second—and without thinking of honor. As for me, honor has to be of the utmost importance: I am an authentic Lebanese woman in every sense.

Just as I was thinking about honor, my oldest brother suddenly entered my unlit room. I imagined that he was carrying a submachine gun in his hand, aiming it at my head and shooting me with one round after another, piercing my skull, exploding and splattering my brains on the wall behind me. The strange thing is that this scene was very familiar to me; I felt that I had witnessed it somewhere previously, and not only once but many times.

My brother wasn't carrying a machine gun, but instead some bootleg DVDs of Egyptian films, and he had come to ask me if I wanted to watch them with him. I declined, asking him to leave my room right away and not to bother me; he did as I asked, without protest, though he was clearly irritated.

After he left, I tried to sleep once again, but imagining the possibility that I could be pregnant stopped me. I decided to buy a pregnancy test the next day, though I wasn't brave enough to buy one myself. I called Yasmine to ask her to bring me one, but her mobile phone was switched off.

I thought about calling Yana, but I changed my mind right away.

I realized at that moment that I wouldn't be able to sleep unless I stopped thinking and I wouldn't be able to stop thinking unless I slept, so I put an end to this situation by taking a sleeping pill. While I was waiting for the pill to start working, I thought really hard about Yana. And Yana was the first thing on my mind when I woke up the following morning and stood in front of the mirror as usual.

Just then I noticed that the Coca-Cola advertisement had completely disappeared from the billboard planted in the ground right in front of my window. For the first time in six months the advertisement wasn't reflected behind my own image. Instead the shiny metal that the billboard was made of was reflected in its place, and I felt a strange sense of relief! Indeed I felt as though I had spread my wings to soar high in the blue sky! But just as quickly I bumped into the buildings that obstructed this great expanse of blueness and I got caught on the electrical cables that stretched between the buildings. Yasmine put an end to my flight by entering my bedroom without knocking on the door and saying, "What happened?"

I asked myself, "How did she know?"

But I thought about it and realized that there's no way that she could know because there's no way that she could see something invisible, and what had happened at the Coca-Cola offices is something that no one would dream of happening. No doubt she's asking me, "What happened?" because she found me looking strange—the kohl around my eyes had run all the way down to my neck, leaving traces of tears on my face.

When Yasmine repeated her question, I decided not to tell her about what had happened, and answered her by saying, "What do you mean?"

But I realized that I had made a mistake in my choice of answer because my appearance gave me away and lacked the nonchalance that I was trying to affect. I immediately regretted it—disavowing that anything had happened only confirmed to Yasmine that something momentous had occurred. She walked over to me, held my face between her palms, bringing it right up close to hers, and whispered, "Abeer, tell me what happened!"

After she promised me that she wouldn't tell Yana, I told her everything, bursting into tears that overflowed right out of me, my snot and saliva both streaming onto her clothes. Once the tears had relented a little, she took me to the bathroom, washed my face, rubbed the kohl from my eyes, combed my hair, changed my clothes, and then said, "You have to tell her!"

I responded, "Are you crazy?"

But Yasmine said that she wasn't crazy and that she was sure that Yana wouldn't be angry with me if she knew about this, instead she would come to understand my situation, especially if I told her that what happened in the Coca-Cola Company was against my will and wasn't my fault. I interrupted her, saying angrily, "I might be pregnant by him!"

I asked her to go to the pharmacy and buy a pregnancy test for me. She asked me first thing when my period was due and I told her that it wouldn't come for another two full weeks. She said that a pregnancy test can only be used after your period is late, not before it's due, and so I had to wait until the day my period was due before I could use such a test to know if I was pregnant! I told her that I wanted to get one in any case and keep it with me, and I repeated my request that she go alone and buy me one, for fear that someone who knows me would see me in the pharmacy and tell my father about it. But she insisted that I come with her, telling me that she would take me to a faraway place where no one would know me and no one would know my parents. The faraway place was Jal al-Deeb. When we arrived at one of the pharmacies located on the main street, Yasmine got out of the car and I stayed in my seat to wait while she went and bought the test. But she came over to my side and opened the car door to let me know that I should get out. So I followed her. As I was walking the distance between the car and the pharmacy, I wished that I had put on a wedding ring before leaving the house. I said this to Yasmine but she ignored me, opened the pharmacy door and said firmly, "Go on, go ahead in."

I wanted to protest but the voice of the pharmacist sitting inside prevented me, asking us to close the door so that the air conditioning wouldn't escape. We entered the pharmacy quickly and closed the door behind us, keeping the cold air inside.

I hid behind a shelf with beauty preparations lined up on it so that the pharmacist wouldn't notice me. I asked Yasmine to go over and ask him for a test, but she grabbed me by the hand and pulled me behind her so that we came right up to where he was sitting behind his desk in the back of the pharmacy. He asked us what we wanted. What we wanted, as Yasmine said in English, was: "A pregnancy test, please." The strange thing was that she said this with genuine nonchalance, as though she were buying a kilo of cucumbers from the little shop owned by her neighbor Abu Said, for example, and not a pregnancy test! Then she specified for the pharmacist the brand of the test that she wanted and I asked myself, "How does she know that?" I waited silently until she paid for it and then I followed her outside.

In the car, Yasmine grabbed the box with the test and waved it in my face, saying: "What? Did somebody murder you?" And I responded, "If I had bought a pregnancy test from the pharmacy across from my house somebody would've murdered me for sure!"

Yasmine laughed but I scowled at her and put the box with the pregnancy test in my purse so that no one would see it. I kept the scowl on my face the entire way to her place in the Snoubra area. And when we entered her building, I was aware that her neighbor Waleed wasn't standing in my way this time.

After Yasmine opened the door to her place and we went in, she got ready to lock it right away as I took the box out of my purse. I found that it consisted of two tests and I decided to use one of them immediately to set my mind at rest. When I told Yasmine I was going to do this, she seemed irritated and replied, "Do what you want!"

I headed for the bathroom, pulled down my underwear and sat on the toilet. After a few seconds, Yasmine came in and kissed me on my forehead and then she left, shutting the door behind her. I shouted out all of a sudden, "Wait!"

She came back to the bathroom right then. I asked her not to leave me alone, so she stayed with me and without hesitating watched how I peed on the pregnancy test. The test showed that I wasn't pregnant, and I would have jumped for joy had I not noticed at that very second how dangerous this would be. My underwear was down around my ankles—something that could have made jumping fatal if I had stumbled, fallen, and bumped my head on the edge of the toilet tank or the tub. I had to put my underwear back on before I could jump to express my joy, but after I had gotten dressed, I changed my mind and was content just to smile.

But Yasmine didn't smile; she frowned and reminded me that this result was meaningless—I could still be pregnant. Then she offered to take me to the gynecologist and get me an ultrasound of my uterus, which would instantly reveal with total accuracy whether I was pregnant or not. I told her that going to the doctor was out of the question because there was a huge risk that this could lead to even more shame and disgrace. Yes, it could lead to a giant disgrace in the fullest sense of the word! Could Yasmine even conceive of what would happen to me if my family found out about this? No doubt they would chop me into pieces—they would chop me up in the very same Moulinex mixer that I had once given to my mother for Mother's Day!

I was vehemently angry when I said this because I couldn't understand why she wasn't being more understanding about my situation. And the more I talked, the angrier I grew until I almost exploded with rage, like a cholesterol-clogged artery... but Yasmine suddenly cut me off, saying very simply, "Calm down, Abeer! This isn't a matter of life and death!"

I didn't say anything back, but I thought, "Fine, let her say what she wants!" I thought, "So I've got no choice then, except to wait until my period's due and the blood flows out of me like Coca-Cola bursts from a can that's been shaken before it's opened! And I'll just have to wait for this flood and hope and pray!"

This was the first time in my life that I had longed for my period to come. After a few hours of waiting, I was filled with anxiety and doubt. I was looking at all the angles, or at least most of the angles, of the situation and I began appreciating its seriousness, i.e., the seriousness of the possibility I could be pregnant! For the past two days, I'd been feeling that everything was an irritating dream—impossible that this could be happening for real, and to me of all people!

After those few hours, the wait began to feel very long. I felt that the two weeks standing between me and my period were an eternity. I attempted to shorten this eternity just a little by passing my time in front of the television. I thought that this would allow me to kill two birds with one stone (if that were possible of course, from a purely practical point of view), because firstly, television makes time pass faster and secondly, it would distract me from thinking about my period, pregnancy, and Yana. It would help me forget my troubles because my mind would be on pause until it was time to confront them.

This attempt failed, however; in fact it totally fell apart. The television didn't make me forget my troubles, but actually did the opposite—it constantly reminded me of them because Yana was always appearing on it. Every time I saw Yana on screen I changed the channel, as though I were trying to escape being infected by a deadly microbe.

Yana had started appearing on television lately as one of the dancers in a video clip that had been shot a few months before and had come out recently. The song the video was made for had been hugely successful and the clip was being broadcast nonstop on every TV station.

The song was so successful because it was basically an old and very famous song, "Didi" by the Algerian Rai singer Cheb Khaled. It was re-released by a German pop group called *Milk and Honey*. This group was made up of two women: one of them was nicknamed *Milk*, and was blonde, her skin white like milk; the other was nicknamed *Honey*, her darker skin almost honey-colored.

I remembered sadly that *Milk and Honey* was the very name that Yana had called Yasmine and me and for the very same reason. Yasmine is as white as labneh and I am dark, closer to kibbeh-colored, fried kibbeh, of course! Or maybe a little less dark...

I also remembered that Yana had told me once that she decided to call us this after she had heard a song by the group *Milk and Honey* for the first time; she fell in love with the song from its very first note. She saw in its opening lines the most beautiful description of her first meeting with her boyfriend, as though these words were written for none other than the two of them:

On a dark desert night, in a land far away
You took my heart—that's the price I pay.

These opening lines inspired her to think about eternal, tormented love in a dune-filled desert where date palms flourish!

I remember that at the time I had asked her, "But how is tormented love related to sand dunes and date palms? And what do sand dunes and date palms have to do with Lebanon—where you first met?"

I added that I was born in Lebanon and have lived here my entire life and I've never seen any sand dunes, except those shown on television or depicted on boxes of dates imported from Saudi Arabia and Iran. Moreover, how could she talk like this—after all the time that she's spent here, after all she's seen? At the end of the day, she lives above a Starbucks, of all places!

She tried to come back with, "I am free! I want to dream!" in Arabic. But she turned her "h" into a "kh," so instead said something like, "I am shit! I want to dweam!"

When I remembered all this I realized that I really missed Yana and that I hadn't seen her or spoken to her for a few days, something I wasn't used to at all. This nostalgic longing is what finally prompted me to watch the entire *Milk and Honey* video, despite the amount of pain it would cause.

I watched it and found it really beautiful. This was the first time that I had seen it.

The video begins with a wide shot of a sweeping desert that at first glance basically looks like a plate of hummus. The expansive, never-ending sand dunes are golden like crushed chickpeas and a small orchard of date palms in the middle of one sand dune is green like parsley leaves placed in the center of the plate of hummus as a decoration. As for the ancient stone castle in the center of the orchard, from far away it resembles the chickpeas that are in turn placed on top of the parsley as another decoration. After remaining on this shot for a few moments, the camera begins gradually to zoom in on the stone castle, in order finally to go inside of it, where the two singers are standing between marble columns in a spacious entry hall, singing.

The director must have added this desert/hummus scene using digital effects, because they filmed this video clip in one of the old Beiruti houses in an alley off Gemmayzeh Street, not in the heart of the desert as this video makes it seem! I know this because I went with Yana on location to the filming.

This location wasn't exactly what the director wanted, so afterward he added some things to the video digitally. For example, he wanted to film the small fountain in the center of the entry hall overflowing with fresh water. But the family who owned the house told him that they hadn't used the fountain in many years because the water pipes were so worn out. He kept insisting, so they deferred to his wishes and opened up the pipes to let water flow into the fountain. A sticky, brown-colored liquid emerged from the fountain and they immediately went and turned it off. He also had wanted to film a scene that would show this house's windows, but he discovered it would be impossible because the glass was broken in a number of places and the gaps were covered by plastic bags, stuck onto the glass with Scotch tape.

The director changed all of this in the video, which showed the glass of these very same windows as colored and covered in inscriptions and drawings. As for the fountain: pure, sparkling, clean water gushes out of it. The moment I saw this I said to myself, "Computers can bring the dead back to life!"

At the very same time, I felt a kind of pride, because the house where they filmed it is a Lebanese house, located in none other than Beirut itself! Today this house appears on German, French, English, and American television screens where people, sitting in the living rooms of their houses on the other side of the globe, daydream about a world that looks like paradise... a far, far-away world.

I also felt proud because my friend (or should I say my former friend?) participated in creating this work. She appeared in front of the camera constantly, but only in the background, behind the two German singers, who themselves were almost hidden beneath the gold bracelets, anklets, earrings, and necklaces that they were wearing—they could have collapsed at any moment under the weight of all that gold! But they held on, as though the weight of all this gold were no burden at all, and performed their belly dancing with great elegance. They seemed to defy the laws of gravity, especially the blonde one who moved her body and hands so quickly that at times her arms almost seemed like the blades of an electric fan.

I noticed that just about in the middle of the video the blonde woman sang one sentence in broken Egyptian Arabic, a sentence that was almost incomprehensible because her pronunciation was so bad. Immediately after, the two women said together, in French, *"Habibi, je t'aime, Tu est mon roi et je suis ta reine!"*

They both said the word "habibi" exactly how Yana used to say it to her boyfriend.

The moment that I heard the way they pronounced this word, I remembered that I might be pregnant and, after all of this drawn-out reflection on Yana, this was the straw that broke the camel's back—I couldn't control myself any longer and I just burst into tears.

A short time after I had calmed down, Yasmine walked right into my room without any prior warning, as usual. When she saw traces of tears on my face she told me that I needed to turn off the television that minute and get out into the world to forget my troubles! According to her, the best way to forget these troubles was to go with her to the gym where she boxes.

I declined her offer, so then she insisted, saying that I should learn to box as soon as possible, so that I could possess at least the minimum knowledge of fighting techniques, which is very important because then I would be able to defend myself when I needed to.

She told me that this sport was the reason why she could push the guy off of his motorbike when he tried to get into our car that time, when we were taking Yana to her gynecologist's appointment. She, as a matter of fact, could punch any man and squash him... like an insect! Yasmine said this in all seriousness, very excitedly, and then stomped the heel of her foot on the ground, emphasizing her strength and in particular her ability to squash things. At that moment I wanted to tell her that squashing insects is no longer tantamount to physical strength, especially after the invention of insecticides like Piff-Paff, for example, which kills them very easily with only the press of a button. Therefore her comparison of a man to a squashed bug is a thing of the past. But I restrained myself because Yasmine was extremely excited and emotional.

"If you had known how to defend yourself, what happened to you wouldn't have happened!"

I don't know if this argument is what finally convinced me to go with her to boxing practice. But as soon as I conveyed to her that I was convinced, I immediately regretted saying it, since I realized after only a few seconds that my agreement to box in itself was an indirect agreement to receive painful, damaging punches, all over my chest and indeed all over my face—most boxing punches, as Yasmine once told me, were specifically aimed at the face, and this scared me! When I expressed my fear to her, she told me that there was no reason at all to be afraid and that today she would train me herself before it was time for her to train with her team, that way I wouldn't be forced to face an opponent or receive any punches. So I was reassured and we went together to the gym.

We went on foot because the gym was located off one of the little side streets in Mar Elias near my house. We set off in the evening when the electricity had been cut, as it usually was at this time, so the neighborhood streets were enveloped in darkness.

This was the first time that I had dared to walk there at night; normally, I would avoid this, out of fear of the young men who always gather at building entrances. But today I didn't feel any fear because I was with Yasmine.

When we finally arrived at the gym, we went into the training room and I turned to look at a guy who was wearing bright pink boxing gloves—a color that Yasmine really hates, she says it disgusts her, that in her opinion it's a symbol of exaggerated femininity. This boxer's legs were shining like a brilliant, polished Pyrex dish, something that invited commentary from one of his teammates, who teased him, "Legs so long and lanky… Whoa, that bitch is skanky!" He then added, "Did you wax recently?"

I couldn't hear his answer—at that moment Yasmine pulled me into the room next door so that we could change into our boxing gear. When we entered this room, I felt an urgent need to use the bathroom and asked Yasmine where it was. She laughed and said that there's no women's bathroom in the club because it's a men's club! She added that I could go in the men's bathroom when none of them were in it, but I turned down this suggestion, preferring to hold it until I went back home. Yasmine supported this decision, saying that waiting was much better than rushing into something, and me going into the men's bathroom would really be rushing into something because this bathroom was a germ's paradise, a paradise with sewage streams flowing below it!

She said this then took off her bra, in front of one of the mirrors hanging on the room's walls and started examining her breasts. After a few seconds, she took some lotion and started rubbing it onto them, saying, "Oh, they're lost in a haze, the olden days…"

I asked her what she meant and she said that she missed her breasts, eradicated by time! Only a year or two ago they had bloomed with life, like a gorgeous garden! Now they have melted away and almost disappeared completely. The reason for this, she said, was her excessive boxing practice: she moved her arms so much in this sport that she'd burned off all the fat in her chest and her breasts kept shrinking. In trying to restore her breasts to what they had been previously, she'd bought this cream from an herbalist, hoping it would encourage life in them and get them to grow again.

But she had discovered after a period of using this cream that it was useless, and that her breasts did not respond to the breath of life as they should have. They were like a wilted flower that it was impossible to make blossom anew. She applied it assiduously, however, because she still held onto a small margin of hope.

Yasmine sounded profoundly distressed as she told me all this!

While she was talking, I looked at her naked breasts, which really were very small. In fact, they would be almost completely flat were it not for the two nipples that stuck up out of her chest like nails sticking out of a wall. When she finally put on her jersey, her nipples showed through the cloth clearly because she didn't wear a bra.

When we left the changing room and went into the main training room, some of the boxers noticed Yasmine's nipples and started staring at them. But she paid no attention to this, kept acting normally, as though it were nothing, and started to teach me some of the basics of boxing. Shortly after we started this training of ours, some of the other boxers gathered around and started to stare at us. This energized me and I concentrated, trying to apply everything she'd been teaching me: I hit the punching bag with all my might and was astonished by how much I enjoyed it.

But one thing disturbed this unbridled pleasure of mine—I remembered Yasmine's naked breasts and I was scared that my breasts would become like hers, two nails sticking up out of a wall. I imagined that with every punch I landed, I was getting closer and closer to this destiny! For this reason I was relieved when we had to end our training and stop punching the bag, because Yasmine's coach had entered the room to announce that it was time for boxing practice.

I was really surprised when the coach came in because the coach was a woman who was around four months pregnant!

This woman told the boxers, who were lined up in front of her like soldiers, that they would spar against each other today, then she sat on a chair near the wall, resting her hands on her swollen belly.

In the middle of the training session, the coach noticed the owner of the pink gloves hitting his opponent on the head with the inside of his hand. Clearly she thought that his blows were too weak because she screamed at him, "Ali, punch more powerfully! What do you think you are, a cabaret dancer?!"

Ali followed her advice, but it didn't work out exactly as she meant—he broke the jaw of his opponent, who then had to be rushed to the hospital. But Ali, like all the other guys, reduced his power significantly when it was his turn to face Yasmine. She tried to take advantage of this situation and landed a powerful punch on his face, its sound echoing in the room like a sharp smack. This increased her zeal and she tried to repeat this glory by following up her punch with another one like it, but Ali stopped her attack with one punch to her face, which jolted her as though she had been stunned by an electric current!

Blood poured out of her nose and her eyes filled with tears, but she didn't cry. She wiped the blood from her face and asked her coach to let her stop the match, which the coach allowed.

Yasmine rushed toward the changing room, and when she passed me, I got up from where I was sitting and followed her. When we entered the room and shut the door, she told me straight away—without me saying anything—that the only reason all that had happened was that her period was about to start, which overwhelmed her body and impeded her ability to tolerate pain! This meant that she wasn't able to complete the match and had to stop competing. I didn't respond, but nodded my head to signal my agreement. I wanted to wind up the conversation and leave the gym as quickly as possible—my bladder was about to explode!

Luckily, I was able to get home a few seconds before that explosion happened.

After I went to the bathroom, I went to my bedroom and fell asleep immediately, feeling totally shattered. I wondered, could this exhaustion be one of the signs of pregnancy?

I woke up the next morning and, when I went to look in the mirror as usual, I stopped to look at the image of Yana reflected behind my own image, also as usual. But I had forgotten that the Coca-Cola advertisement had been removed from the billboard the day before and so I was surprised this morning when in its place I saw another ad, for the company Exotica.

This advertisement reminded me that a few months ago Yana's modeling agency had nominated her to be one of a group of models Exotica would consider for this ad. Exotica didn't choose Yana, choosing instead the model whom Yana no doubt considered her main adversary, even though Yana would never openly acknowledge this. Yana clearly took Exotica's rejection as a great loss, despite her pretense at the beginning that she was chosen to be in the ad but had turned it down. She maintained this pretense, until as a result of my own insistence I found out that her competitor was chosen instead of her and I asked her, "Why don't you just admit you didn't get the job? Do you think you have to appear in every single advertisement?"

But I immediately regretted having said this, because I was her friend and I should have been a source of strength for her and not the opposite, especially since the model who was chosen was much more beautiful than her, at least in my opinion. Yana's competitor's striking beauty was really bewitching in this ad, across the bottom of which was written: "Beirut, Umm al-Dunya." Yasmine came to visit me a few days later, noticed the advertisement and really liked it. She especially liked the words written below the picture, "Beirut, Mother of the World." In response I asked her, "If Beirut really were a mother, indeed if she were even a woman, would she been worried about cellulite?"

But I noticed by saying this I had annoyed Yasmine, so I changed the subject and asked her how Yana was doing. She told me that Yana had started her new job in the hotel a few days ago, but she was forced to miss work today because she had to go to the Central Security Office to renew her expired work visa. I said, "She'll spend the whole day there for sure!"

And then I said to myself, this is my chance to go to Hamra Street without the risk of running into Yana! The day I'd learned that my cousin Hala was getting married, I had decided to go to the tailor who made all of Yana's clothes to have him make me a dress to wear to the wedding. But since then I hadn't had the courage to do it because the shop was too close to Yana's house. So, no sooner did I find out that she'd be out of the neighborhood then I headed straight for the tailor shop, with the sign above its entrance announcing, "Nezar the Tailor: A Poet in Clothing Design."

Under this sign, in small print like the Ministry of Health's warning label on a box of cigarettes: "in his hands, you will become... a poem!"

So I asked the tailor, "Will you make me into a poem, then?"

He smiled and asked me my name; I answered, Abeer Ward, Fragrant Rose! He responded, "Your beautiful name shows that you're already a poem just as you are!"

His praise made me happy, but I just as quickly remembered that I didn't like my name.

Nezar asked me what I wanted, and after I told him, he inclined his head to lead me to the middle of the room, where he started taking my measurements. He started with my hips and I noticed that his way of taking measurements was completely different from the norm. Rather than standing behind me and wrapping the measuring tape around me, then gathering up the two ends of the tape on my back, he stood in front of me and encircled me with his arms, leaning forward so that his long nose touched my chest very slightly. Then he gathered the ends of the measuring tape from behind and his fingers touched my rear end.

It seems that he didn't like my hip measurements

the first time, because he asked me to suck in my belly and not to breathe before he measured them again in the exact same way as before. When he had finished taking all the measurements, he asked me to come back a week later. I thanked him and left.

A week later, on the day of my appointment with Nezar, my period came, and I started to believe in miracles! When the blood flowed out of me, I felt that it was life-giving rain pouring down from the heavens! The sharp pains were an enormous relief, enough to assure me that I wasn't pregnant and that everything would go back to normal, exactly as it should be, on the straight path with no potholes or pitfalls. I loved this pain, but despite this newfound love, I took painkillers just as I usually do.

When I went to the tailor, I discovered that the first day of my period is not the right day to be fitted for a dress. When I went to try on my dress, Nezar looked at my swollen abdomen and said, "What's this?"

If I wasn't so shy, I would have explained that my abdomen bloats during my period and it's impossible for me to suck in my belly as I usually do. But instead I just took the dress and silently went to try it on. The dress was tight because of my huge belly and after I zipped it up I felt that the blood from my period would be pressed out of my uterus like lotion being squeezed out of a tube.

I could feel blood violently bursting out onto my pad! This great burst was accompanied by an even greater amount of pain.

I ignored the pain, left the changing room and stood in front of the tailor, who leaned over and started folding the edges of the cloth at my feet and putting pins in to get the length of the dress right. While he was doing this, his head was directly facing my pubic region and his long nose had almost slipped between my thighs! At that moment I remembered what Yana had once told me about the smell of sanitary pads saturated with blood, which she could smell from a few meters away! I feared that the tailor's long nose would be as efficient as Yana's, especially since Nezar spent a long time down on his knees in front of me with his nose directly facing the origin of the odor!

I tried to encourage him to hurry up and finish his job but I wasn't successful. When he finally got up and stood in front of me, it seemed as though he had an evil smirk on his face.

The look on his face angered me so much that I decided then and there to exchange my foul-smelling sanitary pad for a tampon, and I thought of going immediately to Starbucks (not the pharmacy) to buy one from the machine on the bathroom wall.

The moment I left the tailor, Yasmine called me and told me that she had just been to my house and didn't find me there, so I told her to come and meet me at Starbucks. Then I went into the café, where a young employee was carrying a tray filled with plastic cups the size of Arabic coffee cups, the kind Starbucks always uses to distribute free samples of a new drink before it's released onto the market. The young man said, "Take one, Madame!"

But I didn't take one, because I didn't realize that I was the "Madame" that he meant; I didn't even consider that these words might be directed at me of all people. I wasn't used to anyone calling me "Madame," indeed I was used to "Mademoiselle," which is how one addresses single, well-bred, virtuous girls! I considered myself one of these girls, so I immediately assumed the waiter's remark must be directed at someone else, a lady who would fit the title "Madame," and for whom it would be more appropriate. However, this other lady wasn't there, I was standing alone in front of this young man. When he repeated his words more clearly, in a louder voice, it became obvious that the intended "Madame" was none other than me... and I was shocked!

I came undone just like a puzzle when it is broken apart and in just one second transforms into a pile of tiny, individual pieces!

I asked myself, "How did he know?"

How did this young man know that I was no longer a "mademoiselle"? What made him declare this so openly and confidently? I drew the following conclusion: Since this young man addressed me as "Madame" so easily from just one look at me, this must mean that there's some sign that I've lost my virginity stamped on my forehead, like an expiration date stamped on the bottom of a package of food, which anyone could read. The man who sells mana'eesh on the corner near my house will read it, for example; my grandmother, who doesn't even know how to read, will read it. My father will read it!

My father, who always says to me, "We are the Ward family, the Roses, and you, Abeer, are our Fragrance!"

At that moment, all of my father's sayings and proverbs showered down on me like rain—acid rain, of course!

All this took place within seconds while the young man was still waiting for me to take a cup from the tray. I didn't take anything, and instead turned my back on him and ran to the bathroom. In the bathroom, I started crying, until I remembered that crying would smear the kohl around my eyes, and I stopped. But I didn't leave, for fear that someone might see my face flushed red from tears and I preferred to wait until it cooled off a little and the redness went away.

A few seconds later, one of the young women from the café entered the bathroom and I went right into one of the stalls, closing the door so that she couldn't see me. Then I lowered the toilet cover and sat on it. This left me facing the bathroom door, which I was used to seeing always covered in writing and drawings, and today I was surprised because it was completely blank! The door had been stripped of all these writings and then covered with white paint until it was snowy white and gleaming like a sheet in an advertisement for laundry detergent. I couldn't stand that whiteness and I took my stick of kohl out of my purse to write something on the door—but I changed my mind.

Then I decided not to leave this toilet stall before I found a way to reorder my life, which had scattered all around me like so many puzzle pieces. I found the solution to my problem instantly, as though it had descended from the heavens by email—this solution was to restore my hymen. This seemed to me a completely appropriate and proper way to rebuild what had been destroyed in my life, and I opened the stall door to go out into the main part of the bathroom. At that very instant, Yasmine entered the bathroom, and I told her about my decision. She responded, "Have you lost your mind?" When I didn't answer, she added, "The restoration operation is pointless because everything that you're going to restore you'll just go and break again!"

I felt insulted and I told her so. She didn't answer and thought a little bit before saying, "Why the hurry? You don't have any immediate plans to get married in any case!"

She was right about that.

I nodded my head, and at that moment remembered that I had wanted to put in a tampon instead of a foul-smelling sanitary pad, but I changed my mind and left the bathroom.

Just then, my mobile phone rang; it was Yana and I didn't dare answer it. I realized that I needed to talk to her face to face and decided to meet her the next day to tell her about everything. I told myself, "Definitely, I'll talk to her tomorrow!"

But I didn't talk to her the following day, because I couldn't find her. I tried to call her many times but her mobile phone was switched off. When Yasmine called I asked her if she knew anything about Yana and she replied in the negative. The next day, I went to her place and didn't find her there, but instead found the building's workers busily refitting the tiles. I asked them about her and they replied that they didn't know anything but they also added that she must have moved because this house was being converted into an office.

A few days later, I received a long email from Yana, informing me that she had returned to Romania, and telling me the reasons for this sudden departure.

To start with, she said that she had lost everything the moment she got pregnant: she lost the job that supported both her and her family, she lost her boyfriend and she lost all hope that he would come back to her and marry her—all of this made her think about returning to her own country. But she didn't decide to leave Lebanon for sure until the day she went to the General Security Office to renew her expired work visa and she was shocked at how one of the employees there treated her. When he learned that she was residing in Lebanon as an "artist" (this is what was stamped in her passport), he burst out laughing.

This was the last straw! At that very moment, Yana headed straight for her ex-husband's place and asked him for a document giving her permission to leave the country before their divorce was completely finalized; he gave her what she asked for with no objection. Then she bought her ticket, packed her suitcases and left Lebanon that very same night!

She left with no regret or sorrow, yielding to what she considered to be her qadar and nasib—fate and fortune!

Then in the last lines of her message she mentioned that she still loves Lebanon and that she will return one day because she wants her child to get to know his father's country. She emphasized that we must stay in touch and meet again—but without specifying when this meeting might be!

At the end of the message, below her name, she added,

"*PS*: Give Hala my regrets since I won't be able to attend her wedding and tell her that, if she wants, now she can serve tabbouleh!"

Translator's Afterword

The translator's confession: when the author of *Da'i-man Coca-Cola* read the first version of its translation into *Always Coca-Cola,* she hated it. After a late-night Skype phone call, in which we both were politely frustrated with the other's opinion, Alexandra Chreiteh sent me an email, "Please don't hate me but…" that crossed in cyberspace with mine, "I think that we can work out our differences but…"

And so our conversations about the translation of this short novel began, leading to a long process of discussion about not only the specifics of this text but also translation theory, politics, and practice from our different and overlapping positions—as author and translator, teachers, students, readers, writers—between Lebanon, the United States, and Canada. I will not detail all of the intricacies of our conversations about the translation process that created *Always Coca-Cola*, this English-language version of Alexandra's Arabic-language novel. I would instead like to use this afterword to outline several of the major issues that were a part of these conversations.

The purpose of this translator's afterword is not to offer the reader an explanation or analysis of the novel. Rather, I hope in these few pages to reveal some of the processes that affected its move from Arabic into English. My work here is informed by a keen awareness that all translations are mere readings and interpretations, offered by someone who has worked carefully and extensively with the text, of course, but nonetheless always subjective and never definitive. My goal in creating *Always Coca-Cola* has been to try to convey to the reader the sense of the narrative and story of this novel, while also giving a flavor of how it works in the Arabic and the kinds of linguistic play Chreiteh uses. I want to allow *Always Coca-Cola* to live and grow in its English-language incarnation and to have the kind of English-language "afterlife" that translation theorists like to talk about.

One of the elements that makes *Always Coca-Cola* so difficult to translate is its deceptive simplicity and familiarity. At first glance, it might seem easy to translate a work with a straightforward plot, a great deal of description of familiar things, and that draws upon so many referents and concepts that are well-known globally. From the title itself—a marketing slogan for Coca-Cola, perhaps the ultimate expression of globalization—to the characters' preferred café, Starbucks, to their conversations about boys and sex, dating and marriage, tampons and gender roles, this novel resonates with the current issues and concerns of young women and men all around the world. Its edgy and cynical humor of twenty-something college students is recognizable across languages, cultures, and geography.

Several challenges are posed by this "familiarity," by the novel's global resonance and recognition. Firstly, the surface similarity on display in *Always Coca-Cola* in fact masks larger differences. One of the elements that I find so brilliant within this novel is that it is not a story that simply could be taking place anywhere—the very specific and particular bourgeois West Beirut milieu of young women at the Lebanese American University (LAU) is constantly being invoked and satirized. Rather than drawing upon the signs and symbols of global capital in a superficial way, or to make the text "accessible" to a supposed Western audience, *Always Coca-Cola* draws on them in order to make larger comments about the specificities of the local scene, surroundings and world view of her characters, who are very much part of a Lebanese reality. One of Alexandra Chreiteh's concerns when we started discussing the translation was that the novel was too specific and limited to a very particular milieu. Would an English-language readership understand her invocations and gentle mocking of these places and symbols?

The second major challenge that I faced is one that confronts every translator of Arabic. How do you represent the different registers and levels of the Arabic language in English? One of the contributions of this short novel to the contemporary Arabic literary scene in Lebanon is its innovative use of language: the author employs Modern Standard Arabic to express things most often not recorded in this formal language. This is the literary language used in most writing practices throughout the Arab world; it differs from the "everyday" language that people speak. The language that girls speak together when gossiping or that mothers speak to their children or that lovers whisper to each other is usually not the language that is written down in newspapers or books. Like many other contemporary Arab authors, such as Rachid al-Daif, Iman Humaydan and Hanan al-Shaykh, Chreiteh experiments with a simplified version of this language—with a few instances of the colloquial language being mixed in—and uses it to narrate events rarely recounted in such language.

This is a contribution that the Arabic version of *Always Coca-Cola* makes that cannot be adequately replicated in English. The example that always occurs to me is when Yana goes to the beauty salon and Abeer describes every step of her Brazilian wax in excruciatingly lurid detail. In the translation of this scene, I did not use the expression "Brazilian wax," even though this is the immediately obvious, "fluent" translation of what she was having done at the salon. I made this choice consciously partly in order to try to address the question of the original work's experimentation with language. In the Lebanese colloquial Arabic spoken in the milieu being described, women would simply refer to this as a "Brazilian" much as in English. In the novel, Chreiteh uses a formal Arabic word "aana" which more precisely means "pubic area" to describe the part of the body being waxed. This is a rather neutral, formal word that is neither used in everyday speech in Lebanon nor has crass or vulgar connotations. She repeats this particular word over and over again. My translation choice here was to remain slightly detached and formal, as the language of the original text does—though for different reasons in the Arabic version—in order to recreate its formal linguistic structure.

A parallel but opposite process is at play in one of the other very difficult translation choices that I made. What is the best way to capture the interruptions of local Lebanese expressions and jokes in this more formal, standard language? These lines are ironic, often rhyme and are impossible to translate in a way that feels satisfactory. The process of working with these moments was the most fun part of translating—I asked everyone I know for suggestions and had many people at work coming up with improbable rhymes. Jokes were exchanged, I learned new English-language slang from my students, much of it inappropriate to record here, and learned more about Lebanese Arabic. The most obvious example of this comes right near the end of the text when Yasmine and Abeer go to the gym to train for a boxing match. Some young men are making fun of another one who has his legs oiled up for the match and say to him, in Lebanese slang, "Shu hal-sahbeh ya ahbeh?" (or written in the common "texting Arabic" used among young people today, in which letters missing in English are replaced with numbers: "Shu hal-sa7beh ya 2a7beh?"). This expression rhymes and is meant to be funny. It comments on the "sexy legs" of the young man, while calling him a derogatory term for a woman, something the equivalent of prostitute, whore, bitch, or slut.

This expression posed a number of problems. The first and foremost was the rhyme. How can you capture an Arabic rhyme with an equivalent English expression? Then, it inverts another, similar rhyming expression which compares a man's body to a lion, complimenting his masculinity, "shu hal-jasad ya-asad?" But in the expression we were working with, a term had to be found that makes fun of a man, invoking gendered language that implies that he is like a woman, but gently and in a joking spirit. After much debate I decided that "bitch" was the right word and spent months trying to rhyme it with an appropriate expression that would compliment his legs. After a period during which I changed my mind and had all but settled on the contemporary slang "'ho" instead of "bitch" (for 2a7beh) because of its greater rhyming possibilities, my students provided me with a wealth of choices from which I finally settled on "Legs so long and lanky, whoa that bitch is skanky."

One final difficult issue, amongst many more that I will not detail here, is: How can you capture a dialogue in English that is completely written in Modern Standard Arabic but that is meant to represent people speaking English? The characters in the novel are all meant to be speaking English most of the time. Because Yana is Romanian and Abeer and Yasmine are Lebanese and they study at an English-medium university, English is their common language. In fact, Yana's mispronunciation of Arabic is also referred to frequently in the text and is the source of many jokes.

These moments are difficult to convey because they are not very funny in English—her mispronunciations are not immediately apparent and have to be explained, losing some of the comic effect. My solution to this is to sometimes embed descriptions in English in the translation that explain some of these contexts. I have tried to keep these to a minimum because my overall translation strategy is to leave the original text to speak for itself through my interpretation as much as possible.

As a translator, of course, invoking my conversations with the author gives my own work a certain authority. But implying that I have Alexandra Chreiteh's "stamp of approval" on the finished version does not put an end to the questions that we both have about the translation. Indeed we still do not necessarily agree on every translation choice that I have made. In the final version, I was particularly concerned with preserving elements of strangeness and difference in the text; this is rooted in my concern with how texts often lose their specificity and character in the move from Arabic to English, particularly in our contemporary English-language political and cultural climate of the beginning of the twenty-first century. This often trumped Chreiteh's authorial desire to make the text as accessible as possible to an English-reading audience. Originally, she wanted the text to read as fluently as possible and I was strongly committed to preserving an "Arabic accent" in a text moving from Arabic to English, from a Lebanese literary context to an English-language one. I was concerned with the importance of the power dynamics when Arabic texts move into English, leave their "local" setting and enter a "global" one. Because of the Arabic text's play with language, humor, and irony, I was particularly worried about losing this and creating a homogenized text that would be appealing but lose its edge. The result is a compromise, but one which I largely controlled. I thus take responsibility for where this translation may be difficult or less readable, while gratefully acknowledging Alexandra for pushing me to think differently and to create a text that we both can live with; hopefully, it is better because of our collaboration.

Translator's Acknowledgments

For her generosity of spirit, cynical outlook, and wicked sense of humor, I would like sincerely to thank Alexandra Chreiteh. I want to acknowledge Michel Moushabeck and the people at Interlink Books who make it possible to work in creative and collaborative ways on translation, not always common in today's marketplace. Special thanks are owed to the painstaking and conscientious work of Hilary Plum. Once again, Elise Salem facilitated my path to translating a novel from Lebanon, merci kteer. A grateful acknowledgement to colleagues and friends who helped me with specific words and passages— Malek Abisaab, Khalid Medani, and Laila Parsons. Thanks also to Rachel Galanter and Amanda Hartman who read it in English (on vacation) and thought with me about words and phrases. I would also like to thank enthusiastically the students in my translation seminar at McGill University, fall 2010, who pushed my thinking on the politics, theory, and practice of Arabic–English translation; they helped me to solve some of its trickiest problems: Hussam Ahmad, Jay Alexander, Chloe O'Connor, Jennifer Dunn, Katy Kelamkarian, Gayatri Kumar, Rachel Naparstek, Elizabeth Snyder, Julia Wilk. The biggest thanks go to Dima Ayoub, who worked as more than just a research assistant on this project. She discussed the entire translation with me more than once and helped in obsessing about many of the issues, problems, passages, as well as specific word choices and overall framework. It is her translation too. A very large debt is also owed to the women whose work allowed me to finish the translation: Alison Slattery, Marie Lippeveld, and Mama Rachel Zellars. As always, my parents deserve bigger thanks than I can give in print for their ongoing practical and emotional support. Yasmine Nachabe was also a crucial support and interlocutor in Beirut during the final stages of finishing this translation, thanks to her and the other Taans.

This translation speaks to generations of girls and young women; working on it transported me to my own university days, some of them spent in Beirut. In this spirit it is dedicated to the women I spent those years with, most importantly to my sister, Amanda.